D0492115

Anne Fraser's new duet
Doctors to the Stars
has the inside scoop on stories
the paparazzi can only
dream of uncovering...

DOCTORS TO THE STARS!

Amongst the glitterati of the rich and
famous, cousins Fabio and Kendrick are
infamous for their heart-stopping good
looks and dangerously tempting charm...

By day Fabio is a top-notch Harley Street
doctor—by night he's an adrenaline junkie
who's utterly irresistible to women!

Kendrick, the unstoppable stuntman for the
world's biggest Hollywood blockbusters,
leaves broken hearts on every film location!

*But Fabio and Kendrick's roguish ways
are about to be tamed...!*

**Book one,
THE PLAYBOY OF HARLEY STREET,
is also available
from Mills & Boon® Medical™ Romance
this month**

Dear Reader

Welcome to the next two books in my mini-series *Doctors to the Stars*!

I love writing about strong, alpha men who like to test themselves to the limit and in this book I have two of them. Thrill seeking cousins Fabio and Kendrick share a love of extreme sports—and women.

Enter Katie and Elizabeth, two women who are grieving and definitely not looking for romance. But just as it looks as if they have found love with two men who have issues of their own, life still has one more curve ball to throw their way.

Despite the difficulties associated with writing about bereavement and life-limiting illness, especially when children are involved, I had so much fun writing these books and I really hope you have as much enjoyment reading them.

I have tried to make sure the medical information is as up to date and accurate as possible. However, since I wrote *The Playboy of Harley Street*, there has been progress in the treatment of cystic fibrosis. Very good news for sufferers and their families.

Anne Fraser

DOCTOR ON THE RED CARPET

BY
ANNE FRASER

MILLS
BOON®

First published in Great Britain 2011
by Mills & Boon, an imprint of Harlequin (UK) Limited.
Large Print edition 2012
Harlequin (UK) Limited, Eton House,
18-24 Paradise Road, Richmond, Surrey TW9 1SR

© Anne Fraser 2011

ISBN: 978 0 263 22423 8

Printed and bound in Great Britain
by CPI Antony Rowe, Chippenham, Wiltshire

Anne Fraser was born in Scotland, but brought up in South Africa. After she left school she returned to the birthplace of her parents, the remote Western Islands of Scotland. She left there to train as a nurse, before going on to university to study English Literature. After the birth of her first child she and her doctor husband travelled the world, working in rural Africa, Australia and Northern Canada. Anne still works in the health sector. To relax, she enjoys spending time with her family, reading, walking and travelling.

Recent titles by the same author:

THE DOCTOR AND THE DEBUTANTE
DAREDEVIL, DOCTOR…DAD!†
PRINCE CHARMING OF HARLEY STREET
RESCUED: MOTHER AND BABY
MIRACLE: MARRIAGE REUNITED
SPANISH DOCTOR, PREGNANT MIDWIFE*

The Brides of Penhally Bay
†*St Piran's Hospital*

CHAPTER ONE

DR ELIZABETH MORGAN stepped out the car, transfixed at the hustle and bustle in front of her. The desert heat of California smothered her skin like a blanket, making her damp blouse stick to her back. Rivulets of perspiration trickled between her breasts.

What was she doing here? She glanced wistfully at the driver as he unloaded her suitcases, tempted for a moment to tell him not to bother. She'd made a mistake, changed her mind—would he please take her back to Los Angeles International Airport? And straight onto a flight back to England.

But she couldn't do that.

Wiping the dust from her face with a tired hand, Elizabeth took a deep steadying breath. Right—the director must be somewhere amongst the crowd of people. Dragging her cases behind her, she picked her way along the rutted dusty ground, her feet throbbing in her unsuitable high heels. This wasn't what she'd expected. Weren't all movies made in a studio? Not out in the back of beyond near Palm Desert in what must be a rundown mining town. Hardly the glamour and sophistication she'd envisaged.

Not that she could bring herself to care. It was all she could do these days to put one foot in front of the other. If it hadn't been for the fact she'd known she would go crazy if she stayed in London, she would never have taken this job. Doctor on a Hollywood film set was as far away from what she used to do as it was possible to get. At least here there were no constant memories of the life she once led. And that was its attraction.

She screwed her eyes up against the harsh midday sun. Filming was in full swing, it appeared. Cameramen were perched high on top of mobile cameras, people stood in clusters, talking animatedly, and around what appeared to be the central filming area, large aluminium caravans stretched almost as far as the eye could see.

Just then a horse cantered by, kicking up dust and with someone clinging precariously to its neck. Elizabeth watched, heart in mouth, as the rider seemed to lose what little balance he had and slid further off the horse, before landing with a thump on the ground.

Elizabeth paused only to pick up her medical bag. Judging by the way the rider had fallen, he was bound to be badly hurt.

But to her amazement, before she had even crossed the few yards to his side, the man was on his feet, wiping dust from his trousers with a nonchalant flick of his cowboy hat.

'How was that, Philip?' he called out in an American accent. 'Was that realistic enough for you?'

Elizabeth slowed to a walk. He was big this man, well over six foot and powerfully muscled. He was wearing faded jeans that clung disconcertingly to his thighs and cowboy boots with spurs. He had short brown hair and a wide mouth and had such an air of masculine assurance about him that instinctively Elizabeth knew this was a man who broke hearts. Was he one of the actors? Silly question—he was bound to be.

He stopped swatting the dust from his clothes as she approached, and gave her a long slow stare. Then he grinned, showing even white teeth. If he carried on riding horses like that, Elizabeth thought testily, he wouldn't have perfect teeth for much longer.

'Howdy, ma'am. I don't think we've met. I'm Kendrick,' he said, holding out his hand.

Elizabeth's fingers were enveloped in his. For some reason the way he was looking at her was making her heart race. Then again, she *had* got a fright. She'd really thought that the way this man had fallen from the horse meant she would be fixing him up and calling an ambulance. And all before she'd even unpacked.

'Dr Elizabeth Morgan,' she replied. 'I'm the doctor for the set. Are you all right? Maybe you should sit down.' She glanced around. The only place she could see was a couple of camping chairs outside a trailer a few yards away. What if he collapsed before she got him there? She'd never be able to support a man of his size. 'Actually, back on the ground will do while I look you over.'

His grin grew wider. 'Now, come to think of it, ma'am, I think I did hurt my shoulder. Maybe you should have a quick look-see?'

Before she could say anything he whipped off the dust-smeared cambric shirt he was wearing, revealing a bronzed chest with a number of scars. His torso was muscled, not overly so but enough for Elizabeth to be able to detect each individual ridge. He wore his jeans low on his hips, and his abdomen was taut, with a fine sprinkling of dark hair disappearing into the waistband. She blinked.

This was a man who was perfectly aware of the effect he had on women—other women that was. He'd find out soon enough that she was immune to any man.

'I really do think you should sit down, Mr...?' she said. The ridiculous way her pulse was behaving you'd think it was her who had just fallen off a horse.

'It's Kendrick. No one calls anyone here by their last name. You might be all formal in England...' He raised an eyebrow at her. 'You are from England, right?' When she nodded he continued. 'But we all use first names here, Lizzie.'

'It's Elizabeth. And I'd prefer you to call me Dr Morgan,' Elizabeth responded stiffly. When he quirked an eyebrow at her she flushed. Damn the man. Everything about him made her feel at a disadvantage. 'Now, which shoulder did you hurt?'

He stepped closer until he seemed almost to block out the sun. She resisted the impulse to move away.

'Come to think of it, the shoulder is fine. I was kidding.' His eyes glinted down at her.

'I'd rather you didn't waste my time, Mr...er... Kendrick,' she said, dismayed at the way her heart continued to race. 'You've heard about the boy who cried wolf, haven't you?'

Her words only made his smile wider. He turned to call over to a middle-aged man with long side-burns and a ponytail who was making his way towards them, accompanied by a young woman in the tiniest denim shorts Elizabeth had ever seen.

'Hey, Philip. We have someone over here who likes fairy-tales. Maybe you should explain who I am. I have a feeling this little lady isn't going to believe a word I say.'

Just who was he calling a little lady? Who did he think he was? Was he so absorbed in the movie he was acting in that he was getting it confused with real life?

The man he called Philip sauntered towards them with the girl in denim shorts, who was taking short, fast steps in outrageously high heels as she struggled to keep up with him, all the time passing him pieces of paper to sign as they walked.

'Okay, Sunny, that'll do for now,' Philip said. 'I'll catch up with you after lunch.'

Sunny?

The girl shot Kendrick a look from under thickly mascara'd eyelashes. Kendrick winked back, earning himself a blush before Sunny tottered away on her high heels.

'You must be Dr Morgan,' Philip said. 'Glad you made it here so quickly. I'm the director.' He waved a hand towards Kendrick. 'I see you've already met our stuntman and stunt co-ordinator. 'Kendrick, Dr Morgan has stepped in for Dr Marshall. You might want to keep on the right side of *her*, seeing as you're likely to need her services at least once during this movie.'

Kendrick flung his shirt over his shoulder and smiled again. 'You know I don't tend to get hurt, Philip, that's why you employ me.' Kendrick tipped his head at Elizabeth. 'Good to meet you, but if you'll excuse me I should get washed up.' With a casual wave of his hand he turned on his heel and strolled away.

There was silence as Philip and Elizabeth watched Kendrick's retreating back.

'He's right, you know. He rarely gets hurt—at least not seriously. But there's always the possibility. That's one of the reasons we need a full-time doc on set,' Philip said. He looked at Elizabeth. 'I'm sorry I wasn't here to meet you when you arrived, but nothing interrupts filming when we have the right light I'm afraid. I'm glad you were able to fill in for Dr Marshall at short notice.'

Elizabeth wanted to know what had happened to Dr Marshall, but decided not to ask. She would find out soon enough.

'Why don't I show you around then you can get settled in?' Philip said. 'I'll explain what it is we need you to do on the way.'

'I'd appreciate that.'

'The film we're shooting is an action movie, but you might have gathered that. It involves car chases, horses, a few explosions. That sort of thing. Kendrick does most of the stunts, although we have some others, including a stuntwoman. You'll meet her later. I understand that you have experience in emergency medicine?'

'I've completed training in emergency medicine.' She wasn't going to remind him that it had been a couple of years since she'd worked as a doctor. It was all in her CV. Besides, some things you never forgot.

'Good. A lot of what you'll do here is deal with sore throats, upset stomachs, fairly minor stuff, although at times you'll think your patients are at death's door from the way they complain. Having said that, I'm counting on you to keep our cast and crew healthy. Any time they have off costs the production serious money.'

They walked across an open stretch of ground and into a dusty street lined with wooden buildings. Elizabeth wondered if they were real or just facades. If so, they were remarkably authentic in appearance.

A tumbleweed rolled past. The heat was intense.

'We have our two stars, Jack and Tara, as well as about twenty other actors. Add in the supporting staff, camera crew, sound recordists, grips, runners and film extras and that takes the number to around a hundred. We'll keep you busy.'

'I'm glad to hear it,' Elizabeth responded honestly. Busy was exactly what she needed, and the busier the better.

Philip paused in front of a large tent. 'Most of us eat here together, but you have a kitchen in your trailer so it's up to you what you choose to do.'

Elizabeth nodded. Although she would have preferred to keep out of everyone's way when she wasn't treating them, she knew it would be difficult in such a small community. She didn't mind eating communally every now and again as long as nobody asked her too many questions. While she was here she intended to do her job and keep herself to herself.

'Okay, that's more or less it,' Philip said. 'Except for the medical trailer, where you'll work out of. It's on the other side of the camp. It's equipped with everything you could need. Anything serious, God forbid, we send into LA by chopper. There's always at least one available.'

'I'd like to see the medical facility now, if that's okay. Just to check that everything is there that I'll need.'

'Sure. I think you'll find it's better equipped than some small hospitals. Like I said, we can't take any risks with our cast, and that includes Kendrick. After you've had a look around, I'll ask Sunny to take you to your trailer, so you can settle in. You'll meet everyone at lunch or on the set. Filming starts again at two p.m. We'll need you to hang around for that. We're going to be shooting some stunts with Kendrick and knowing him there's bound to be a scrape or two that will need attention.'

Philip left her to look around the medical trailer, telling her that he'd send Sunny to take her to her accommodation. He had been right when he'd told her money hadn't been spared when it had come to fitting out the facility and Elizabeth was impressed. It was so well equipped she could probably deal with most scenarios. There was a defibrillator, monitoring equipment, basic drugs—just about everything she was used to having when she'd worked in a hospital.

And when Sunny returned to take Elizabeth to her caravan—or trailer as the Americans called it—it seemed no expense had been spared there either. Sunny had hurried off again as soon as she'd shown Elizabeth where she was to live for the next few weeks.

It was a relief to step out of the blazing sun and into the air-conditioned mobile home. A compact kitchenette was fitted with every mod-con and device ever thought of. Swinging open the cupboard doors, Elizabeth noted they were fully stocked. Did she have Sunny to thank for that? Comfortable couches lined three walls of a living room dominated by an enormous plasma-screen TV. DVDs and books filled a floor-to-ceiling bookshelf.

Slipping off her shoes, Elizabeth opened the door leading off the sitting room and found a bedroom complete with double bed and wardrobe. This was certainly a far cry from the cramped caravans she remembered from childhood holidays. It was more like a five-star luxury suite— with an en suite bathroom to boot. And someone had thoughtfully brought her suitcases in for her as well.

Maybe this wasn't going to be so bad after all.

Elizabeth reached into her handbag and retrieved the photograph of her daughter, placing it carefully on the bedside table. She touched a finger to her lip, then to the image.

'Morning, darling,' she whispered. 'Bet you never thought you'd find Mummy in a place like this, did you? I only wish you could be here with me.'

Elizabeth's throat tightened as she trailed her fingers over her daughter's face. No amount of longing or praying or wishing could bring the precious child in the photo back to life and into her arms.

Dragging her eyes away, she glanced at her watch. There wasn't time to unpack before lunch and filming, but she definitely needed a quick, cooling shower and a change of clothes.

Afterwards, feeling refreshed and slightly more human, she redid the plait in her hair, changed into a pair of white cotton trousers and a T-shirt and stepped outside, screwing her eyes up against the midday sun.

Kendrick rotated his shoulder and winced. Damn it. The fall had hurt him more than he cared to admit. He watched the new doctor come out of her trailer and whistled under his breath. She was a stunner. Even with her long blonde hair captured in a plait and wearing a simple white T-shirt and low-slung cotton trousers, anyone could see that she had a body that could drive a man crazy. Add the aristocratic nose and the cool, almost icy blue eyes and Kendrick knew she would be a challenge. But what the hell? That was what made her interesting. Years of dating women from all walks of life had honed his instincts and already he suspected that Dr Elizabeth Morgan might be his toughest challenge yet.

Elizabeth put a few pieces of fruit and cheese on her plate and looked around the mess tent for a place to sit.

She'd hesitated about going for lunch. She hadn't had much of an appetite over the last couple of years and the last three months had put paid to the little appetite she did have, but she knew she had to eat. She couldn't risk getting ill. She had no doubt, and neither could she blame them, that the film company would replace her in a heartbeat if they felt she wasn't up to the job.

However, she almost changed her mind when she arrived at the dining tent. It was crowded and she couldn't see an empty seat. As she was about to retreat back to her trailer Kendrick appeared by her side, his plate piled high with grilled chicken and rice. Unlike her, it seemed as if he had a pretty good appetite.

Catching her look, he grinned. 'Protein. Good for repairing muscle, isn't it?'

Elizabeth shrugged. 'Doesn't look as if you have much problem in that regard.'

When his grin widened, she realised that she had spoken without thinking. 'I mean…you assured me there was no damage after your fall,' she added hastily, annoyed to find she was flushing

'Tell you what,' he drawled, 'why don't we find a place to eat outside in the shade? It will be more comfortable, apart from anything else. The fans they use to try and keep the air circulating in here aren't much good.'

She didn't want to have anything more to do with Kendrick than she had to, but as she opened her mouth to refuse she saw that he had already turned away to go back outside. There was nothing she could do without seeming rude except follow.

He was right, there was more air outside. Moreover, a little breeze had come in from somewhere, cooling her overheated skin. Kendrick pulled out a folding chair for her, before easing his long, powerfully built frame into one beside her.

'So, tell me, Lizzie, what brings you here?' he

asked, forking a piece of meat. 'All the way from England? I would guess London if I had to narrow it down.'

She noticed he was no longer speaking like a cowboy from a movie. In fact, despite the American accent, she could have sworn he had spent some time in the UK.

'You're correct,' she said. 'London. But I spent some time in America before...' She bit her lip. She didn't want to go there. She didn't want to talk about her life back then. She definitely didn't want to think about Simon and she couldn't bear to think about Charlie. 'Before going back to the UK,' she finished lamely.

Kendrick studied her thoughtfully for a moment.

'What about you?' she asked, before he could ask her anything else. 'If I'm not mistaken, you've spent time in the UK too.'

'And you'd be right. I went to boarding school in England. My parents travelled a lot and my mother is English. But we were talking about you.' Kendrick neatly turned the conversation back.

'Nothing much to tell.' At least, nothing much she wanted to tell. 'I went to medical school— St Bart's?' She raised her eyebrows in question.

When he nodded, indicating he knew it, she continued. 'I trained in emergency medicine and then worked with the London Air Ambulance service for a year. That's about it.'

'Married? Kids?' His eyes dropped to the bare finger of her left hand. Elizabeth sucked in a breath.

'I was married but it didn't work out,' she said evenly. This was exactly the kind of conversation she wanted to avoid.

'I'm sorry.'

'Don't be. It happens.' She placed her plate to the side. 'Isn't it time for filming to start again?'

'It'll probably be closer to two-thirty before it gets under way. Our leading lady isn't known for her timekeeping.'

When he smiled at her, his eyes creased, revealing faint laughter lines. She wondered if everything amused Kendrick.

'In that case, I guess I'll go along to the medical trailer. There might be someone who wants to see the doctor before filming starts.'

'Do you know where it is? I could show you if you like.'

'Philip took me there earlier. Anyway, don't

you have to be on set, getting blown up or something like that?' she said, more sharply than she intended. The trouble was, and she didn't know why, this man was getting under her skin, despite the fact she had just met him.

Kendrick looked baffled. He stood up, slapping the dust from his trousers.

'Sorry, Lizzie. I hope I didn't say anything to offend you.'

Elizabeth felt herself go cold with embarrassment. He was right. Despite his blatant interest and the way he looked at her, he'd been friendly and welcoming. He wasn't to know that she was barely holding it together. That since Simon had left her, she'd erected a shield around herself. And then as Charlie had become sicker and sicker... A wall of pain slammed into her and she swallowed hard.

None of that excused her appalling manners. Kendrick wasn't to blame for any of it.

'I'm sorry, that was rude of me. I'm just a little...' she struggled to find the right word '...out of sorts, that's all.'

The ready grin flashed, but before he could say

anything, a loud screeching noise made them both whirl round.

'What in the name of…?' Kendrick said.

Philip was using some sort of megaphone in an apparent attempt to summon the cast.

'He needs to get that thing tuned.'

As they shared a smile, Elizabeth's heart missed a beat. He had the devil in his bright blue eyes, she thought irrationally.

'Have to go, I'm afraid,' Kendrick said, sketching a salute. 'We're going to need you too. Philip has been putting off this scene until you got here.'

'What kind of scene?'

'I have to drive a car off a cliff.' The matter-of-fact way he said it made it sound as if this was what most people did as a part of their daily routine.

'Oh, really?' she said with a lift of her eyebrow. He had to be winding her up again, but this time she wasn't going to fall for it.

'Don't worry. I jump out of the car once it goes over the cliff. I'm not actually in it when it hits the ground. Or at least I hope I won't be.' He muttered the last few words.

'Let me get this right,' Elizabeth said. 'You are

in a car that goes over a cliff, but you jump out in mid-air? And how do you get back on the ground? Fly?'

'It's not as difficult as it sounds. They've removed the rear window. Once the car goes over, I climb out and sort of sky-dive to the ground. I'll have a parachute.'

She still didn't know whether to believe him. It sounded too fantastic.

But as the trucks, loaded up with cameras, cast and crew, including Elizabeth, rolled out into the desert coming to a stop at the top of a cliff, she realised that Kendrick hadn't been teasing her.

Philip was hustling everyone to get into position. 'We don't have much time, folks,' he said. 'And I don't want to do this more than once, so let's get it right.' He turned to Elizabeth. 'You better check with Kendrick where he'd like you positioned, just in case he has a problem.'

Elizabeth nodded. This was why she was here and she needed to be prepared for anything. Heaving her medical kitbag over her shoulder, she searched around for Kendrick.

Given his height, it wasn't difficult to spot him amongst the crowd of people. Although the set was buzzing with noise and activity, she could hear his distinctive voice coolly instructing his team above the clamour. As if he sensed her gaze, Kendrick looked over towards her. As their eyes locked, her pulse missed a beat. This was a man totally in control and completely in charge. What would it be like to have someone like him on your side? Someone to count on?

Almost immediately, Elizabeth shook the thought away. Where had that come from? She didn't really know anything about Kendrick. There was no way she was ever going to go down that road again. He was just a man, a work colleague.

She threaded her way amongst the crowd until she was standing in front of him.

'Where's the best place for me to wait in case I'm needed?' she asked.

He gave her a lopsided grin. 'Lizzie, if this goes wrong, no doctor is going to patch me up.' His voice grew serious. 'Not that anything will go wrong. But with a stunt like this, other factors come into play, so we have to be prepared for anything. We're cordoning off a safe area at the foot of the cliffs. Watch out for falling debris when the car falls to the ground—that's the biggest risk to the crew.'

'Okay.' The words 'Good luck' hovered on her lips, but she bit them back. Somehow she didn't think Kendrick would need it. Instead she made her way over to the base of the cliff and behind a toughened plexiglass screen. He'd certainly thought of everything.

From the bottom, the cliff looked even higher. Kendrick was right. If he didn't manage to get out of the falling car in time, or if his parachute failed, she doubted she'd be able to do much to help him. There was a very real possibility he could be killed. Her blood ran cold. But he was a professional. This was what he was trained to do.

After a tense hour and a half they were ready. The car rolled over the lip of the cliff and into space. An explosion splintered the sky, sending sparks of dazzling yellow and orange outwards and sizzling towards the canyon floor. A collective gasp went up from the onlookers, but still the cameras kept on rolling. After what seemed like an eternity, but could only have been a second or two, a figure clambered out of the rear window and launched itself away from the falling car. Elizabeth couldn't have pulled her eyes away even if she'd wanted to. There were a few heart-stopping seconds as the figure fell, hurtling towards the ground, and there was no sign of Kendrick's parachute opening. Elizabeth tensed, positive that the sound of the car crashing to the ground was going to be followed by the thud of his body. Only when his parachute whooshed open did she realise she'd been holding her breath. Kendrick landed lightly on his feet, several metres away from the burning wreck and only a short distance from her.

He sketched a bow as everyone applauded.

Relieved that for this scene at least her services hadn't been needed, Elizabeth crossed over to Kendrick, who was divesting himself of his parachute.

'Are you okay?' she asked.

He turned glinting eyes on her. She could tell that he'd got a kick out of what he'd just done.

'Perfect,' he said.

'That was crazy,' she said. 'I don't know why you let Philip talk you into doing it. No film is worth dying for.'

His eyes narrowed and he frowned at her. 'Relax, Doc,' he said.

Although his tone was light, there was an undercurrent of steel in his words. 'I have no intention of getting myself—or anyone else on my team—killed. We spend a lot of time discussing and planning the stunts beforehand to eliminate as much risk as possible. Then we deal with what's left. It's what stuntmen and women do. If you don't like it, perhaps this isn't the job for you.'

He looked over the top of her head. 'Hey, Josh, Immy. What d'you think? Did Philip get the shot he needed?'

He walked away, leaving Elizabeth feeling dismissed.

Who was he to tell her what job did or didn't suit her? But she had to admit he was right. Her job wasn't to worry about Kendrick or to tell the film producers what they could or couldn't do. Her job was to keep them alive long enough to get them to hospital should anything happen.

Filming over for the day, Elizabeth knew that this was the time that the cast and crew would be most likely to look for her should they require a medical opinion. She took a ride on the first truck heading back to the camp and, sure enough, she was kept busy until dinnertime, seeing members of the crew who had sore throats or sunburn. Nothing too serious and nothing that required more than some painkillers or advice.

When she was certain there were no more patients, she locked up. If anyone needed her out of hours, they knew where to find her.

She let herself back into her trailer and picked up the photo from the bedside table.

Charlie was staring into the camera, a small smile on her face. It had been taken just before she'd lost control of her neck muscles, but even then they had been deteriorating, giving her a lopsided look. But to Elizabeth her daughter looked beautiful.

Elizabeth started to unpack. On top of her clothes was Charlie's favourite soft toy, the ear lightly chewed and missing an eye. A crushing pain squeezed Elizabeth's chest as memories rushed back. Her daughter's little face looking up at her with incomprehension that Mummy wasn't able to help, the feel of her child's tiny frame in her arms as Charlie lost more and more weight. The last time she had held Charlie, knowing that she was slipping away and there was nothing,

nothing anyone could do and that no amount of love or denial could stop her from dying. And then later the small white casket being lowered into the ground, the disbelief that she would have to live out the rest of her life without her daughter.

Elizabeth brought the soft toy to her face and inhaled the still lingering scent of her daughter.

In the weeks following Charlie's funeral Elizabeth had been almost unable to function. She'd wandered around the small house, alone and aching to touch her child. Just once more.

The nights were the worst. She'd find herself curled up in her daughter's bed, soaking the pillow with her tears. But eventually she'd known she had to do something. When she'd seen this job advertised it had seemed perfect. No chance of coming into contact with children, a limited contract that would give her breathing space to decide what to do with the rest of her life, and an environment where people knew nothing of her past and were unlikely to be interested.

As soon as she'd been offered the job and accepted, she'd put her terraced cottage on the market. With a bit of luck it would be sold before she had finished here. With Charlie gone,

Elizabeth couldn't bear to live in the home that had once held such happiness. She didn't know if she could even ever set foot inside it again.

Her throat ached as she remembered sitting on the floor of Charlie's bedroom, tears pouring down her face as she'd packed away Charlie's clothes and toys. She hadn't been able to pack away the soft toy. Together with the photo, it was all she had brought with her to remind her of her darling daughter. Not that she needed anything to remind her of Charlie. Every second of Charlie's too-short life was burned into her soul. She kissed the photo one more time before replacing it on her bedside table.

Although so far her day had been mostly straightforward and the work nothing compared to caring for a severely disabled child twenty-four hours a day, Elizabeth was tired. But for once it was a nice tiredness. She had been able to forget for a few hours. The thought sent another shot of pain through her. Not that she wanted to or could forget her baby. Despite Charlie's disabilities Elizabeth would have given everything she had to have her daughter back.

But that wasn't to be. She had somehow to make some sort of life for herself, even if at the moment she didn't know what that could be.

CHAPTER TWO

THE weather over the next couple of days continued to be hot. The nights were thankfully cooler but still Elizabeth found it difficult to sleep. When she did it was to dream of Charlie.

She was getting to know some the cast and crew. Everyone was friendly and good company. Somehow she was always aware of Kendrick even when she wasn't in attendance for one of his stunts. Often she'd see him walking around the set, joking with the cast and crew or occasionally outside his trailer, his long legs stretched out in front of him. Whenever she walked past him, he seemed to know she was there, even with his hat tipped forward, covering his eyes.

Kendrick wasn't the only stuntperson on set. There was Imogen, who doubled up for Tara, the female star of the film, and Josh, an older man who helped Kendrick with some of the stunts. Gossip on the set had it that Josh had been a rally driver before getting into stunt work and he took the lead in most of the stunts involving high-speed chases. Elizabeth was sure that there was an element of competition between him and Kendrick. As far as she could see, they were always trying to outdo each other in terms of who could do the most difficult stunt.

Most of the filming took place during the day, although Philip had warned her that some of it took place in the evenings, depending on the light.

One morning, Sunny came to see her before filming began.

'I haven't been feeling so good over the last couple of days. I don't know if it's the heat, but I feel as if I have a temperature.'

'Any other symptoms?' Elizabeth asked, taking in the young woman's pallor.

Sunny shook her head. 'Nothing specific. Just as if I'm coming down with flu. And I can't afford to be ill. We're already running behind schedule. If we don't catch up, Philip is going to insist on filming over the weekend and I want to get home to see my kids.'

Grief, Sunny had children? She didn't look old enough.

'Why don't you slip your blouse off while I check you over?' Elizabeth suggested, picking up her stethoscope. 'How many children do you have?'

'Two.' Sunny smiled wistfully. 'Sam is eight and Trixie six. I had Sam when I was seventeen, before you ask.' That made her twenty-five.

'You must miss them.'

'I used to bring them with me on a job and that worked fine until they started school. I could have employed a tutor to teach them on set, but I don't think that's fair, do you? Children need their friends and a routine, don't you think? I want them to have a better start in life than I did.'

Elizabeth's heart tightened as the never-far-away image of Charlie floated in front of her. What she would give to have had her daughter know what having friends felt like. It didn't stop her sympathising with Sunny, though. It had to be tough for the young mother, working away from her children.

'Philip has been good to me. He took me on as a gofer, now I'm his personal assistant. I kind of always hoped I'd be discovered one day, but I guess that's not going to happen now.'

Sunny squinted up at Elizabeth as Elizabeth took her blood pressure. That seemed normal too.

'Do you have children?' Sunny asked.

Elizabeth turned away and sucked in a steadying breath.

'No, it's just me,' she replied, picking up a couple of Vacutainers. It *was* just her—now. 'I'd like to take some blood before we finish if that's okay?' Something seemed a little off, but Elizabeth couldn't put her finger on it.

Sunny nodded. 'It would be good if you could take it where no one can see the marks. Just in case…' She gave a little smile. 'I still haven't given up hope they might use me in the film.'

'I'll try not to leave any, I promise.'

Elizabeth inserted the needle into the crook of Sunny's arm and filled three vials to send to the lab. She didn't think there was anything seriously wrong, but it wouldn't hurt to be thorough.

'I'm really looking forward to seeing the kids next weekend,' Sunny was saying. 'Hey, by the way, we're going to be filming in the studio in Hollywood and Jack is having a party for the cast and crew. I know he was planning to invite you. Everyone else will be there. Even my kids.'

Elizabeth smiled. 'I doubt he wants to invite me, he hardly knows me.'

'Then it's a good way for you to get to know him and the rest of us. He has a huge house on Mulholland Drive—you know, where a lot of Hollywood stars live. His parties have quite a reputation. Half of Hollywood would give their eye teeth to be invited.'

'I'm not really a party animal,' Elizabeth demurred. 'I'm more the kind to go to bed with a good book.'

'In LA?' Sunny didn't attempt to keep the incredulity from her voice. 'You have to be kidding me. Didn't you just tell me that you're footloose and fancy-free?' She nibbled on her bottom lip and studied Elizabeth through violet eyes. She might look innocent, almost naïve, but there was no mistaking the sharp intelligence behind the ditzy exterior. 'Or have you just recently had your heart broken?'

She narrowed her eyes when Elizabeth took in a sharp intake of breath. 'I'm right, aren't I? In that case, you have to come. It'll cheer you up, and who knows—you might meet someone else.'

That was so not going to happen. Never, ever

would she give her heart to someone only to have it broken. The agony simply wasn't worth it. She was finished with men, finished with love. All she wanted now was to find a measure of peace.

'We'll see,' Elizabeth murmured, placing the blood samples into a specimen bag for one of the drivers to take to hospital. 'Okay, I should have the results for you in a day or two. In the meantime, if anything changes, let me know straight away.'

As she was escorting Sunny out of her trailer, Kendrick sauntered up to them.

'Hey, Kendrick, how're you doing?' Sunny greeted him warmly. 'I've just been telling Elizabeth about Jack's party, but she says she's not coming.'

Kendrick eyed Elizabeth. 'Maybe I can change her mind.'

Elizabeth shook her head. 'It's kind of Jack to think of me, but I'm not really the partying kind. I'm quite happy with my own company.'

'I'll leave you two to argue it out, but right now I could do with a lie down. I'm feeling yucky,' Sunny said

Kendrick took Sunny by the arm and turned her

round. He peered into her face. 'You don't look too good. What did the doc say?'

'The *doc* hasn't said very much yet. We think it's a case of flu but just in case, the doc has taken some blood,' Elizabeth said, irritated.

But Kendrick was no longer smiling. 'What about your pee? Is it normal?' he asked Sunny.

Elizabeth was growing more indignant by the moment. Just who did he think he was?

'Well, now that you ask...' Sunny looked embarrassed. 'It's kind of dark.'

An alarm bell went off in Elizabeth's head.

'And when was it that you were in Tanzania for those few days' filming? Ten days ago, if my memory serves me right,' Kendrick continued.

'Yes. About then.' Sunny turned to Elizabeth. 'Philip had a couple of scenes he wanted to shoot there. Something about the light. Only Jack and Tara and a few of the supporting crew were needed, apart from me. Anyway, Kendrick, why are you asking?'

'I think I should have a closer look at you, Sunny,' Elizabeth said. Damn it, she had been so sure it was flu she hadn't even asked the obvious questions.

'Did you take prophylactic anti-malarial medication before you went?' she asked as a confused-looking Sunny let herself be led back inside.

'Yes. Of course. Why?'

Kendrick and Elizabeth shared a look. 'Doesn't necessarily mean anything,' Kendrick said.

He was right. Although prophylaxis helped, it didn't, contrary to what most people thought, mean you couldn't get malaria. Add the flu-like symptoms and the tiredness to the dark urine and malaria was seeming more likely.

'I think you might have to go to a hospital in Los Angeles to be checked out more thoroughly,' Elizabeth said. She could have kicked herself. Why hadn't she asked more questions? 'I should take you there. Is there a car we could use?'

'I'll take her,' Kendrick volunteered. 'I'll use the helicopter. It'll be faster and more comfortable. I could be there and back in a couple of hours.'

'You can fly a helicopter?' Was there nothing this man couldn't do?

'I'm a qualified pilot,' he said briefly.

Elizabeth raised her eyebrows. What was a trained pilot doing working as a stuntman?

'If you could get Philip to agree, that would be

a help.' Elizabeth placed a reassuring hand on Sunny's arm. 'It's best we get you to hospital as soon as we can, but it's only a precaution.'

'I'll tell Philip I'm taking it. Don't worry, he won't try and stop me. I fly it for him for his stunts and we keep it handy in case we need to get anyone to hospital in a hurry.'

Elizabeth guessed that the people most likely to require to be flown to hospital in a hurry would be the stuntmen. Kendrick in particular. She wondered if he'd thought about who would fly him if he got badly hurt.

'The cost of a trip to LA is nothing in the scheme of filming a movie like this,' Kendrick continued. 'Besides, sometimes I fly Tara and Jack to LA for the weekend to save them hiring their own planes. It's all part of the service. We stuntmen do all sorts of stuff on set.'

'In that case, would you clear it with him and let him know what's happening? Sunny, do you want to grab what you need for a couple of nights in hospital? You might want to phone your family and let them know what's happening. While you're doing that I'll speak to the admitting attending at the hospital so they know we're coming.'

By the time she'd spoken to the hospital, Sunny had packed a bag and was waiting by the door of the helicopter. Kendrick was in the pilot's seat, doing some sort of checks, or so Elizabeth assumed.

The helicopter was small with only just enough space for Sunny and Elizabeth in the back.

'Philip's not too happy about me going,' Sunny said. 'He depends on me. Are you sure it's necessary? I don't feel that bad.' Then she groaned. 'Just really, really tired. Is it okay if I lie down?'

'Sure,' Elizabeth said. Sunny was definitely deteriorating. It was good that they'd be at the hospital in thirty minutes.

Elizabeth's stomach dropped as Kendrick took off and she found herself clutching Sunny's hand.

'It's okay,' Sunny mumbled. 'I've see him fly. Believe me, we're in safe hands.'

As soon as they were airborne and the helicopter levelled out, Elizabeth was too busy monitoring her patient to worry whether they'd make it to the hospital in one piece. At least until they got into Los Angeles city and she saw that they were flying just over, and sometimes between, the skyscrapers. At that point she wished she could keep her eyes closed.

Kendrick put the helicopter down so gently Elizabeth almost didn't realise they had landed on the roof of the LA city hospital. Almost before the rotors had stopped turning, the hospital staff were wheeling a gurney towards them.

Sunny opened an eye and tried to protest that she could walk, but she didn't have the energy. Elizabeth quickly updated the doctor, who nodded. 'Don't worry, we'll take it from here. I'm afraid you're going to have to move that chopper from the landing pad. We're expecting another casualty in a few minutes.'

Although she knew the hospital was first class, Elizabeth didn't want to abandon Sunny. But she didn't really have an option. She bent over her patient.

'I'll phone and find out how you're doing as soon as I can.' She squeezed Sunny's hand. 'You're going to be fine.'

Kendrick had hopped out of the pilot's seat in time to hear the doctor's words.

'Jump in beside me, Lizzie. We'd better get out of the way,' he said.

Reluctantly, Elizabeth did as he suggested. She wasn't at all sure about being in front with Kendrick where she had a bird's-eye view of the buildings they had to negotiate their way through, but now was clearly not the time to argue. As Kendrick started the engine he passed her a pair of headphones and indicated she should put them on. Then with another stomach-lurching lift, they were back in the air.

'I should have stayed with her,' Elizabeth shouted above the noise of the engine.

Kendrick winced. 'You don't have to yell.' His amused voice came over the head phones. 'Just speak normally. Sunny will be fine, I promise. Besides, you might be needed back on set.'

Elizabeth couldn't say anything as they flew between the buildings. She was clenching her jaw too tight. Thankfully, and not a minute too soon, they were leaving the city behind.

'How come you guessed it was malaria?' she asked as soon as she could speak.

'Saw a bit of it in the army.'

'You were in the forces?'

'Yup.' He didn't elaborate.

Kendrick surprised her more and more. Thank

God he had recognised what could have turned out to be very nasty for Sunny if she hadn't been sent to hospital.

'I should have picked it up,' she said. 'I can't believe I didn't.'

'Don't beat yourself up,' Kendrick said. 'It happens.

'But not to me. I hate making mistakes.'

Kendrick's smile was back in action. 'I might not have recognised what it was if I hadn't known she was in Tanzania a couple of weeks ago, so I wouldn't call it a mistake, exactly.'

'What would you call it, then?' Elizabeth snapped.

Immediately she felt ashamed. She was tired and out of sorts but that didn't excuse any of it.

'I'm sorry,' she said, shaking her head. 'I'm not usually this touchy. It's just…' She stopped herself just in time. If her history got out, if people knew the real reason she was here, they would be sympathetic and want to know all sorts of stuff she didn't want to talk about. More worryingly, they might wonder if she should be back at work and if she was up to the job. Especially if they knew she had almost missed diagnosing Sunny

immediately. Of course, as soon as the blood results had come back she would have known that
there was something more seriously wrong than
flu. But by then it might have been too late. She
shivered. Sunny had two small children depending on her.

Kendrick was looking at her as if she puzzled
him. It was hardly surprising. Her behaviour must
seem odd at the least.

She forced a smile. 'Thank you for your help. I
really appreciate it.'

Kendrick studied her intently for another
moment, before touching his hand to his head in
an informal salute. Elizabeth wanted to tell him to
keep an eye on where he was flying but she had
the horrible suspicion that if she did, he would
tease her by doing some trick with the helicopter.
It was just his style.

As they flew out over the desert Elizabeth began
to relax. At least out here there was nothing to
crash into.

'It's beautiful,' she said. 'I've never been in a
place quite as desolate as this before, but it has its
own magic.'

'I'll show you more of it when we have time off,' he said.

It was on the tip of her tongue to tell him that she wouldn't dream of spending a minute longer with him than she had to, but she bit back the words. She'd been quite rude enough for one day. It wasn't his fault that he made her feel on edge.

'I'd like that,' she said.

'It reminds me of my folks' home,' he continued.

'Where is that?'

'A few hundred miles to the north. My father has a ranch near the San Bernardino Mountains.' He glanced at her. 'Have you ever been to a working ranch?'

'No. I would love to see one, though.'

When she saw the satisfied smile on Kendrick's lips she could have bitten her tongue. Clearly the man thought he was making progress. Didn't he recognise a friendly, polite response when he got one? But anything she said now would only make it worse.

The rest of the short journey passed quickly. Kendrick made a short detour to point out the San Andreas fault.

'Have you ever experienced an earthquake?'

Elizabeth asked. The thought of one happening, even though they were so close to the fault, didn't concern her. How could it? The worst had already happened.

'I was involved in the rescue mission after the quake in Kashmir. The army used the helicopters' heat-seeking equipment and radar to locate trapped bodies.' He brought his dark eyebrows together and his silver eyes darkened to pewter. 'It was tough. I sure hope we don't see anything like that here, even though they think it's inevitable.'

There was nothing much she could say in reply. The more she knew about Kendrick the more he surprised her. From helicopter pilot to stuntman? None of it seemed to fit. But the closed look on his face told her now was not the time for questions. If ever.

When they touched down they were surrounded by people wanting to know about Sunny. As soon as she'd updated them, Elizabeth excused herself, saying she wanted to phone the hospital, leaving Kendrick to field their questions. Whatever he decided to tell them about her near miss was up to him. Somehow she knew he would make sure there was no blame attached to her and she didn't know how she felt about that. She didn't want to be beholden to this man.

That night, when Elizabeth was lying in bed, her thoughts kept drifting back to Kendrick. Thumping her pillow and throwing off her blankets didn't make any difference. Resigned to a sleepless night, Elizabeth made herself cocoa and took a seat by the window, gazing out at the thousand stars lighting up the cloudless sky.

Earlier she had spoken to the doctor at the hospital and he'd confirmed a diagnosis of malaria.

'Well spotted,' he said warmly. 'A day or two would have made a difference. She would have become a lot sicker. As it is, we should be able to discharge her after the weekend.'

'It wasn't me who spotted it,' she'd said. She couldn't sit back and take credit where none was due. 'It was one of the stuntmen. He was in the army and saw a lot of it there, apparently. He's the one who flew us down.'

'Well, whoever caught it, the result's the same,' the voice on the other end of the phone said. 'But tell him good job from me.'

Why did her thoughts keep returning to Kendrick? There was no doubt he was interesting. One minute he was acting like someone straight out of an action movie, the next he was being kind and perceptive and, she had to admit, good company. But that wasn't the only reason. There was a strength about him, an assurance, as if he was always in control, as if he'd never let anything bad happen on his watch.

In every way he was different from the man she had married. She couldn't imagine Kendrick walking out on his wife and child when that child had a life-limiting illness. But then again, what did she really know about the stuntman? He was clearly someone who liked his freedom. But that was okay. It wasn't as if she was thinking of Kendrick in *that* way. Being intrigued by someone was a whole different ball game to wanting to be with them.

She walked across to the bedside table and picked up the photograph of Charlie. Tracing the contours of her daughter's face with the tip of her finger, she smiled. From the first moment she'd held her daughter in her arms, she'd been overwhelmed with love. In that instant she'd understood when people talked about a mother's tigerish protectiveness. And when Charlie had finally been diagnosed with Gaucher's disease, that instinct had only grown stronger. She would have given her life for her child.

Simon, on the other hand, had been disbelieving, almost outraged. As it had become apparent there was something seriously wrong with their child, he'd insisted on getting a second and then a third opinion. But no matter how many doctors they had seen, the diagnosis had always been the same, as Elizabeth had known it would be. Charlie had inherited a rare gene from both her parents and there was nothing anyone could do to stop the illness taking its course. Finally she had put her foot down.

'Enough, Simon. She has a terminal illness and nothing's going to change that. She won't be with us for long, but whatever time we have with her, can't we just make the most of it? No more treating her like a pincushion. No more dragging her halfway across the world.' Seeing the grief in her husband's eyes, she had softened. 'Let's just love her.'

Simon had shaken his head and looked at her,

his eyes filled with abject misery. 'I don't know if I can cope with all this. I know what that says about me, but I don't think I can.'

And he couldn't. He had tried at first, but soon he'd been spending more and more time away from them and at work. Elizabeth had intended to return to her job with the air ambulance service when the baby was six months old, but that had proved impossible. Not that she'd minded. She'd wanted to make the most of every second she had of Charlie's life.

It shouldn't have been a surprise when Simon had left, but it had been. To be honest, she hadn't even noticed him drawing away from her until it had been too late.

His leaving her rocked her soul, but for Charlie's sake she had picked herself up and carried on. What else could she do? The last time she had seen her ex-husband had been at Charlie's funeral.

She would never love again, she knew that. It was too painful. So why was she even thinking about Kendrick? The man was clearly not her type. But wasn't that part of the reason she was attracted to him? At least he didn't pretend to be something or somebody he wasn't.

CHAPTER THREE

KENDRICK glanced over to where Jack was leaning against one of the cars they were using in the shoot, gesticulating with his hands as he talked. Next to him was Elizabeth but from her body language, arms folded, whatever Jack was saying was cutting no ice. For the first time ever, Jack's famous smile and charm was having no effect. Kendrick eyed Elizabeth speculatively. Most women were fawning, gibbering wrecks when Jack turned on his charm. But Dr Lizzie seemed less than starstruck. Kendrick grinned. The movie star was still persevering, but it would take more than his dazzling, whiter-than-white smile to thaw this particular ice maiden.

What was her story anyway? Why was she so cool and distant? Had she just come out of a broken relationship? It was the most likely explanation for her frosty exterior. If so, he knew exactly how to fix that.

He strolled across to Jack and Elizabeth and was pleasantly surprised to see the look of relief in her eyes when she noticed him and shot him a smile. He loved seeing her all-too-rare smile. It softened her mouth and lit up her eyes.

'Kendrick,' she said. 'Jack was just inviting me to his party next weekend. He says everyone's going.'

Sneaky so-and-so. Trying to get in there first. Thinking that an invitation to his mansion in Beverly Hills would tip things in his favour. His gut was telling him that it would take more than glitz and glamour to impress the doctor, but he wasn't going to tell Jack that.

'You're coming too, I assume, Kendrick?' Although the lead actor smiled, Kendrick could see that he didn't want him to get in his way. Every time they did a film together there would be this little unspoken competition about who would end up with the woman they both wanted. So far the score had tipped in Kendrick's favour, but Jack was only just lagging behind.

'Wouldn't miss it for the world,' Kendrick said easily. 'Would you excuse us for a minute? There's something I need to speak to Dr Morgan about. In private.'

'He's after you, you know that,' he said as soon as Jack was out of hearing.

Elizabeth shook her hand free and glared at him. 'I'm perfectly able to look after myself, you know,' she said coldly. 'And as for Jack *being after me*...' her voice was thick with sarcasm '...I can assure you I'm not interested. In him, or any other man for that matter.'

Ouch. There was no mistaking how she meant that comment. It was time to change tack.

'Look, I was just being a little over-protective. Can't help myself.'

'Not when a little lady might need to be rescued,' Elizabeth bit back.

Wow! She was prickly. This wasn't exactly going to plan. He changed tack again.

'Actually, I wanted to ask you about my arm.' Women couldn't resist a man in pain and as the doctor she had no choice but to take him seriously. 'When I did my latest stunt, I think I wrenched it again.'

Elizabeth's frown was replaced by a look of concern. Kendrick decided not to let the fact it was professional concern bother him. At least she was no longer glaring at him.

'Why don't you come into the medical trailer and let me have a look?' she suggested.

Kendrick raised a triumphant eyebrow at Jack, who was watching them closely, and fell into step next to Elizabeth. 'I'm pretty sure it's just a sprained muscle. Nothing a bit of massage won't help.' He shot her a look. 'I don't suppose you're into massage, are you, by any chance?'

Oops, perhaps he'd overdone it. The glare was back.

'I'm a doctor, not a masseuse!'

She stopped in her tracks and placed her hands on her hips. Kendrick was distracted for a long moment. Her hips curved in just the right places and a man could probably just about circle that waist with the palms of his hands. As for those legs. His eyes travelled down the length of her body and he swallowed a groan as a vivid image of those long legs wrapped around him jumped into his mind.

'When you're quite finished...' a cool voice said, and he dragged his eyes back to her face, only to find himself focusing on a mouth that just cried out to be kissed.

He shook his head. Now was not the place and certainly not the time. Dr Elizabeth Morgan needed a good bit more thawing before he would even risk a quick taste of those lips.

Inside her trailer, Elizabeth instructed Kendrick to sit on her sofa.

Trying to remember that Kendrick's torso was simply a mass of muscle and fibre, she ran her hands over his powerful shoulders. Then she noticed something odd. A star-shaped hole with lines radiating out from the centre just below his left clavicle. Although she had never seen a bullet wound before, there was no mistaking what this was. She touched the scar with her finger.

'Is this what I think it is?' she said softly.

Kendrick nodded. 'Got it in Iraq. Damn bullet chipped a bit of bone. That's what makes my shoulder stiff sometimes.'

Not just been in the army, then, but on active service.

So he hadn't been all together untruthful when he'd crashed from the horse a few days earlier.

A wound like that was bound to cause problems. Especially since he insisted on battering it every day of the week.

'How does a helicopter pilot get a bullet wound?'

His expression darkened and for the first time Elizabeth wondered whether Kendrick was as easygoing as he liked to pretend he was.

'That's a long story. Can we save it for another day?'

This time Elizabeth was sure she saw a shadow cross his face. Did Kendrick have something in his past he didn't want to talk about? Maybe they weren't so different after all?

'Sure,' she said. He was entitled to his privacy as much as she was entitled to hers. Nevertheless, she found herself wanting to know more. Why had he gone from being an officer in the army, someone no doubt with a bright future ahead of him, to a stuntman? And why was she interested? It wasn't as if she was planning to get involved with him. All she wanted to do was to be left alone with her pain. If he had secrets of his own, it was none of her business and never would be.

Turning her attention back to what she was supposed to be doing—giving the man in front of her the best medical attention she could—she carefully felt along his shoulder, probing gently and asking him to lift and lower his arm. There was a little stiffness there, but nothing too worrying. She would like to have a look at his X-rays and medical records, though. Until she saw them she wouldn't be happy that he was working as a stuntman. Repeated banging of a damaged limb couldn't do it any good. She had an idea that Kendrick would somehow have managed to forget to tell the film producers about his medical history.

'Does Philip know about your shoulder?' she asked.

'No. And you're not going to tell him,' Kendrick said firmly.

'He should know. It's not a good idea to carry on working as a stuntman until I see your X-rays. You could damage your shoulder permanently.'

Kendrick's hand shot out and gripped her wrist so hard it was almost painful.

'He's not to know,' he said through clenched teeth. 'You're my doctor and bound by patient confidentiality, isn't that right?'

Surprised by the vehemence in his tone,

Elizabeth removed her hand from his grasp. 'Of course I can't say anything, but I'd feel happier if I could get a look at your medical notes.'

Kendrick eased himself off the couch and picking up his shirt, shrugged into it.

'I have no idea where my records are. Even if I did, there's nothing in them that would give you any reason to worry. Stuntmen work with injuries all the time. If we stopped every time we hurt ourselves, we'd never work. Broken bones and other injuries are part of the job.'

'But not bullet wounds surely?' Elizabeth said sharply.

'No. They don't usually use live ammunition on film sets.' He shook his head in mock dismay. 'That would lead to too many dead actors.'

Elizabeth flushed. For some reason he was always wrong footing her.

'So, what about Jack's party? Are you going to come? Because if you are, we could travel down together.' The teasing look was back in his eyes. 'You don't want to stay here on your own surely? That's no fun.'

Fun? She wondered if she even remembered what that was.

'I'm more than happy to stay here by myself. I happen to like my own company.' She made herself smile. 'Honestly.'

Kendrick eyed her thoughtfully. 'I wonder,' he said slowly. 'At least think about it.'

Then picking up his hat and whistling under his breath he left her feeling as if she'd just done a couple of rounds in a boxing ring.

Kendrick strode back to his trailer.

Trust Lizzie to have picked up on the bullet wound. Despite her anxiety over almost not picking up Sunny's malaria instantly, he doubted she missed much.

He'd liked the feel of her cool fingers on his skin. The way a lock of hair had fallen across her face as she'd bent over. She intrigued him more and more. What was behind that guarded exterior?

Not that he wanted to know, he told himself. His interest in Lizzie Morgan was purely physical. The same as his interest in any woman since Amy.

He winced. Amy. His first love and his last. He would never feel that way again. He wouldn't let himself. Loving someone meant responsibility. Or should do. Their happiness, their life in your hands.

But he had been unable to save Amy. If he'd got there five minutes earlier, might he have been able to? He would never know.

Why was it coming back now? He'd thought he'd closed that particular wound—one that was worse than any physical pain he'd ever experienced. It didn't matter how many big waves he surfed, how many mountains he flung himself off, how fast he rode his horse, no rush of adrenaline, no losing himself in another woman's arms could completely wipe out the feelings of loss and guilt.

If the army hadn't stopped him from flying while they'd investigated, would he have stayed? There was no clear answer to that. Or not one he wanted to think about. At least working as a stuntman gave him a similar adrenaline rush to flying helicopters. He needed his daily dose or he'd go crazy. He grimaced. His father had been disbelieving and furious when he'd told him about his decision to leave the army, but that was too bad. All his life he'd tried to win his father's approval—and failed. Now he was living the life he wanted, with no responsibility for anyone but himself.

He let himself into his trailer and peeled off his shirt, feeling restless and on edge. He needed to be doing something. A workout would help. And after that? An image of blue eyes and a soft mouth jumped into his head. After his workout, he knew just what he needed to keep his head from going places he didn't want to go.

Elizabeth stroked the horse's mane and he whinnied with pleasure. After lunch she had walked around the perimeter of the camp until she had come across the stables.

'You like horses?'

She started as a deep voice came from behind her. She whirled around to find Kendrick standing there. Earlier she had passed him lying on a bench, dressed only in his army pants, concentrating as he lifted weights above his head. Happily he had been too preoccupied to notice her stealing surreptitious glances at him as each muscle in his abdomen and shoulders bunched every time he lifted the weights above his head.

The horse nuzzled its soft mouth into her hand

and she pulled her hand away as its whiskers tick-led her palm.

'Hey, it's okay. Buster won't bite,' Kendrick said, misreading her action.

'I know. I have ridden before.' Okay, so it was years ago and was only once, but he didn't need to know that.

Kendrick raised an eyebrow at her and his mouth turned up at the corners. Elizabeth's heart thumped against her ribs. It would be much better if he wasn't so sexy.

'Have you got anything planned for this after-noon?' Kendrick continued.

Why was he so damned determined to seek her out at every opportunity? Hadn't she made it crys-tal clear she wasn't interested?

'Just work. I'm employed here for a reason, you know,' she said testily, trying to ignore the un-comfortable racing of her heart.

He grinned down at her. 'Not this afternoon you're not. Philip is shooting a close-up that in-volves Jack and Tara in a love scene. Unless some-thing happens there, like she bites his tongue when he tries to put it down her throat, which I wouldn't put past her—they have a bit of history—I think you'll be all right.'

'Why do you want to know?' Elizabeth asked. 'Do you need to see me again? Is your shoulder causing you more discomfort?'

'The shoulder's fine. I thought you might like to come with me to the desert for a ride. We could take the horses we've been using for the stunts. You've already met Buster here.'

Would he ever give up? On the other hand, she hated having time on her own, despite what she'd told him earlier. Without something to occupy her mind there was too much time for thinking, and thinking meant remembering....

'I don't know. It's a long time since I've been on a horse,' she admitted 'I wouldn't be surprised if it had me off in seconds.'

'No, he won't. The horses we use are like lambs—really well trained. Besides, we use western saddles. It's like sitting in an armchair.'

It wasn't just the horses that was making her hesitate. Although she wanted to see what was out there beyond the confines of the set, she wasn't sure why Kendrick was asking her. If he thought she was up for some brief romance with him, he

was very much mistaken. Couldn't he see he was
wasting his time pursuing her?

'It's only a horse ride—I'm not proposing marriage,' he said, as if reading her mind. 'Of course,
if you're too chicken…' He shrugged, leaving the
challenge hanging in the air.

Elizabeth made up her mind. Why not? It was
unlikely that she'd ever be back here, so she should
make the most of every opportunity that came her
way.

'Who do you think you're calling chicken? I've
a clinic to do first, but I can be ready about three.'

She turned away, knowing and having to admit
liking it that he was staring after her. Was she
nuts? Didn't she know that Kendrick spelt danger?
On the other hand, Kendrick was no more looking
for a long-term relationship than she was. In that
respect they were two of a kind, even if for completely different reasons. And she could handle
someone like Kendrick.

The clinic produced no more than the usual
sore throats, sniffles and sore muscles, a sprained
ankle and a paper cut. Despite the work being a
little boring at times, Elizabeth was content that
the cast and crew were keeping well. Especially

after Sunny becoming ill. Although Philip's assistant was very much better, she remained in hospital.

Elizabeth was ready and waiting when Kendrick turned up with a riding hat.

She eyed the hat warily.

'I thought you said it was perfectly safe,' she said. 'I'm not intending to go any faster than a walk. You do know that?'

'Just a precaution,' he said. 'Anyone can fall off a horse. We need to make sure the set doc stays in one piece.'

'Where's yours, then?'

He looked aghast. 'When I said anyone, I didn't mean me. I've been riding all my life and only fall off when I mean to.'

Feeling less certain about the proposed adventure, Elizabeth waited while he fastened the helmet on for her. As his fingertips brushed against her throat, she felt goose-bumps pop up all over her body.

Now that she was committed to riding him, Buster looked bigger somehow and Elizabeth eyed him nervously. Maybe this wasn't such a good idea. But before she could do or say anything,

Kendrick had taken hold of her leg and swung her into the saddle. He was right about that at least. It was like sitting in an armchair.

Kendrick adjusted the stirrups for her, lifting each of her legs in turn while he did so. Elizabeth felt a jolt of electricity each time his hands brushed her calves. Why did her hormones seem to have suddenly come back to life? And why with this man?

Once her stirrups were adjusted to Kendrick's satisfaction, he showed her how to hold the reins in one hand and the pommel of the saddle with another.

'It will make you feel more secure. If you want to go right, just pull the reins to the right and ditto for the opposite direction. You don't have to use your legs—he'll respond to your voice.'

Kendrick swung himself into his own saddle and wheeled his horse round.

'Just follow me.'

As they left the compound behind Elizabeth began to relax, especially when Buster responded to her voice and the slightest pull on his reins. She looked around. The desert seemed to stretch on for as far as the eye could see, with the mountains in the distance. She hoped Kendrick had water in his saddlebags. Of course he would have water. He wasn't the kind of man who would go into the desert unprepared. Risktaker he may be, but idiot he clearly wasn't.

He brought his horse next to hers. 'There's a canyon about five miles from here. I thought we could stop there.'

'Sounds good.'

'How does it feel? Do you think you could manage to post—I mean trot? Or a short canter?'

'I could try.'

'Don't try and rise or anything fancy. Just relax and stay with the horse's movements. I'll go in front. Buster likes to stay behind. If you feel yourself slipping, hold onto the pommel, say whoa and he will. Okay?'

Elizabeth's mouth had gone dry so she simply nodded. Kendrick kicked his horse on to a slow trot and Buster followed immediately. Elizabeth clenched her teeth before remembering what Kendrick had said about relaxing. She forced her body to go with Buster's rhythm and soon she found that it was okay. She could do this. All she had to do was concentrate.

Kendrick was riding with one hand on the rear of his saddle, looking back at her and watching to see how she was doing. If she'd dared let go of the saddle or the reins, she would have given him a thumbs-up. As it was, she managed a smile.

'Want to try a little faster?' he asked.

Not really. This was quite fast enough. But she surprised herself by nodding. Somehow she trusted him completely.

Cantering was more comfortable than trotting had been, even if it felt more like an all-out gallop. She let herself feel Buster underneath her, the way the horse seemed to know what he was doing, as if he wanted to make sure she was all right. After a while Kendrick slowed his horse back to a trot then a walk and Buster followed suit. There was a dodgy moment when the change in tempo made her lose her balance but it was short-lived. As Kendrick brought his horse back alongside hers she grinned at him.

'That was amazing. I loved it. Can we do it again?'

'If you like.' And then he was off again, with Buster following close behind.

They stopped near an outcrop of rocks and

Kendrick jumped down, tying the reins in a knot near his horse's head.

He held out his arms and as she slid off Buster and into them, he held her against him, her feet not touching the ground. She could feel the hard muscles of his chest through the thin material of her T-shirt. Something deep in her belly sizzled. Dismayed, she wriggled until he placed her back on her feet.

'You're a natural,' he said approvingly.

She felt an unexpected stab of pleasure at his words.

He untied the saddlebags from his horse and passed her some water. Elizabeth drank thirstily.

'How far to the canyon?' she asked.

'Another mile or two. If you're happy to canter for some of it, it won't take too long.' His eyes glinted. 'I have to warn you, you're going to be stiff tomorrow.'

They rested against the rocks, which provided welcome shade from the relentlessly hot sun. Unfortunately, for them both to be in the shade meant that they were pressed close together. His jeans-clad leg was warm against hers and doing all sorts of things to nerve endings she'd thought no longer existed.

'So why did you leave the army?' Elizabeth asked. 'I'm only guessing, but I would have thought they'd be pretty keen to hang onto helicopter pilots.'

Kendrick stared off into the distance.

'I guess you could say that the life didn't suit me. I don't like doing what I'm told.'

Now, why didn't that surprise her?

His expression was closed, his eyes shuttered. The message he was giving was loud and clear.

'Why stuntwork, then?' Elizabeth thought it wise to change the subject.

'It seemed the natural thing. My aunt by marriage is an actress. She put me in touch with a director who was looking for someone who could fly a chopper for an army movie he was making. She suggested me. Then they realised I could ride horses too and all kinds of other stuff and I guess it followed on from there. The work suits me. I like the travelling. I like doing stunts. I'm good at it.'

He said the words matter-of-factly. He wasn't boasting. Just saying it how it was.

'What about your folks?'

His expression darkened.

'My father was in the army too. A colonel. He's retired. He works his ranch full time now.'

'Is that how you learned to ride?'

'Yes. I grew up with horses. My folks have always had the ranch.'

There was more to all of this than he was telling her. She was sure of it.

'And you? What about your family?' He turned the conversation back to her.

Elizabeth winced inwardly. Once she'd had a family—a husband and child. Now all she had left was her father.

'My mother died when I was sixteen. My father's pretty frail now. He lives in Canada, although he's American. From the East Coast. That's how come I can work here.'

'Do you see him?'

The last time she had seen her father had been at Charlie's funeral.

'Apart from one brief visit he made to the UK a few months ago, I haven't really seen him for a couple of years.' She hadn't been able to. Taking Charlie out of the country and away from her medical team had always been out of the question. 'But I'm hoping to see him when I finish here.'

'And then? Will you stay in the US or go back to England?'

Elizabeth sucked in a breath. 'I haven't thought that far.'

He was looking at her as if he wanted to know more. She jumped to her feet to avoid further questions.

'Shall we go?'

He said nothing as he packed away the water again. Not wanting to feel his hands on her again, Elizabeth slipped her foot into the stirrup and tried to mount. But the stirrup was too high for her to gain the necessary momentum to swing her leg across Buster's back. When she hit the ground, landing on her backside, she knew she should have waited for help. But she was used to relying on herself. Whatever Kendrick thought, she was no little lady needing some big strong man to protect her.

Kendrick helped her to her feet with a broad grin on his face.

'That didn't go too well, did it?' he teased. 'You should have waited for me to give you a leg up.'

Elizabeth dusted herself off and glared at him. Then she saw the funny side of it and laughed. She'd forgotten how good it felt.

This time, with Kendrick's help, she mounted without further mishap.

They cantered for a while before slowing to a walk again.

'The canyon is over there.' Kendrick pointed with a finger.

Just then Buster reared. It was so unexpected Elizabeth shrieked and dropped the reins. When Buster took off at a gallop, all Elizabeth could do was dig her hands into his mane and hold on for dear life.

'Whoa,' she shouted in the horse's ear, but it had no effect. Buster was making straight for the canyon.

Terrified, Elizabeth was only dimly aware of Kendrick shouting something at her. Probably telling her to pull on the reins. But there was no way she could let go of Buster's mane long enough to try and pick them up. If she did, there was no doubt in her mind that she would crash to the ground.

Suddenly Kendrick was cantering beside her.

He pulled his horse close to Buster, reached over and with one arm pulled her off the bolting horse. It wasn't an elegant manoeuvre—Elizabeth was slung over his saddle like a sack of potatoes—but at least she was no longer being taken towards what she thought would be certain death.

Kendrick pulled his horse to a stop and let Elizabeth drop to the ground.

'Stay here,' he said. 'I need to get your horse.'

Buster, without her hanging on his neck and screaming in his ear, slowed to a canter and Kendrick took off after him. The horse was still heading for the edge of the canyon. Elizabeth didn't know how steep the drop was but it looked as if the horse was heading for certain death. Had she been on his back still, he'd be taking her with him. Did Kendrick know what he was doing? What if the panicked horse pulled him off his mount?

Her heart in her mouth, she watched as Kendrick got alongside Buster again and, leaning forward, almost completely out of the saddle, grasped the reins and pulled both horses away from the cliff edge. Another moment or two and they would have gone over.

When Kendrick trotted back with Buster, who was still rolling his eyes, Elizabeth's legs gave way and she sank to her knees.

'I thought you said he was well behaved,' she cried. 'Like a lamb, you said!'

'Didn't you see the snake?' Kendrick asked. 'The only thing this horse hates worse than tumbleweed is snakes.'

'Now you tell me.'

Kendrick leaped off his horse and came to kneel next to her.

'Are you okay? Sorry I had to kind of dump you back there, but I couldn't risk Buster going over the cliff.'

'I'll live. I guess.'

'C'mon, then. We should get back. It'll be dark soon. Are you okay riding Buster or would you prefer to ride with me?'

If he thought for one second that she was going to get back on Buster he had another think coming. What if there was another snake or, God forbid, a ball of tumbleweed? On the other hand, she didn't want to be so close to Kendrick either.

'Maybe I should walk.'

'Walk? It'll take hours.'

Elizabeth rubbed her backside. Boy, she was going to be stiff tomorrow. 'I think I'd rather walk than get on that horse again. What if there is another snake? There's no way I'm going to go through that again.' She eyed Kendrick suspiciously. 'Are you sure you didn't make him go off? Just to see me make an idiot of myself?'

'Hey, would I do something like that?' Kendrick feigned a hurt look then his face grew serious. 'I wouldn't do that. If you'd fallen you could have really hurt yourself. We need you in one piece. Philip would never have forgiven me if I didn't bring you back safe.'

Elizabeth looked into the distance. The plains stretched as far as the eye could see. Kendrick was right. It would take hours to walk back to the set.

'Okay, Buster, seems you and I are going to have to make this work,' she said into the horse's ear. 'Just promise me that if you spot any more snakes you'll stay calm.'

Grabbing the pommel of the saddle, she heaved herself up, relieved to find that this time she managed to make it without landing on her backside.

After giving Buster a pat, as much to reassure herself as him, she picked up the reins.

'Okay,' she said, pleased that her voice betrayed no hint of her nervousness, 'what are we waiting for?'

They made their way back to the camp at a more sedate pace and with Kendrick taking up the rear this time. As he watched Elizabeth adopt the British way of trotting, he smiled to himself. Had she any idea how cute her bottom was in her tight-fitting jeans? And that wasn't all that he liked about her. He was impressed by the gutsy way she'd insisted on getting back on Buster and riding back to the camp. Most women he knew would have refused point blank.

He was beginning to realise that there was more to Dr Elizabeth Morgan than he'd originally thought, and he was looking forward to finding out more.

CHAPTER FOUR

As she'd anticipated, Elizabeth was so stiff the next morning she could hardly put one foot in front of the other. If only there had been a bath somewhere on set she could have soaked her aching muscles last night and perhaps she wouldn't be feeling like this.

She hobbled over to the mess tent, trying her best to pretend that she wasn't in agony.

But she obviously failed miserably. Kendrick spotted her over the heads of the others and grinned. She scowled at him.

She helped herself to scrambled eggs and toast and found an empty seat close to where the breakfast buffet was laid out for everyone to help themselves.

She winced as her bottom hit the chair. Would she ever be able to sit down again without grimacing? Right now it didn't seem possible.

'Feeling a little stiff?' A familiar deep voice came from her left.

Elizabeth looked up to find Kendrick smiling down at her, his eyes glinting with suppressed laughter.

'I could give you a rubdown later, if you like. It always works for the horses.'

'Very funny and, no, thanks, I'll pass on the rubdown.' Before she could help herself an image of Kendrick's hands kneading her aching muscles flashed into her head and heat rose to her cheeks.

'Don't you have some stunt to do?' She waved her fork in the general direction of outside. If only he'd leave her alone, she might be able to relax a little. Whenever he was around, she felt on edge, as if her body didn't belong to her.

'I do, as it happens. Doing a fight scene with Josh. And then I need to set up Imogen's scene. She has to pretend to fall down the stairs.'

'In that case,' Elizabeth said, 'I'll see you on set.'

The man clearly didn't recognise dismissal when he heard it as he sat down next to her and stretched his long legs in front of him.

'No rush. We have an hour or two to go. Plenty of time.'

Elizabeth stabbed at the food on her plate with her fork. She hated the way he made her feel hot and bothered. In that moment she realised that at least she felt something, apart from grief and a numbness. These last months she had gone through the days on a kind of autopilot.

She didn't know if she wanted the numbness to go away. She didn't want to feel. Feeling was too hard. Charlie's death was like a wound. A wound she needed to leave alone. She had wrapped her heart in ice and she wanted it to stay that way. Thinking about Charlie, her appetite disappeared and she pushed her plate away.

'I have to open the clinic in fifteen minutes,' she said. 'So don't feel you have to keep me company.'

He was looking at her through slitted eyes, as if trying to work her out. Good luck to him. She could hardly work herself out.

'Are you always this grouchy in the morning?' he said eventually. 'I'll have to remember that.'

He grinned again and before she had a chance to think of a retort he jumped up and, catching sight of Imogen, excused himself with a brief word of apology.

Elizabeth found herself following his progress as he walked across the room. Despite his size he reminded her of a cat the way he moved. A panther stalking its prey, creeping up when least expected. He was as dangerous as a wild cat too. Men like Kendrick used women. He would pursue them until they gave in then he would leave them. She knew it with absolute certainty.

She stood too, and dumping her tray on the counter walked as briskly as her tortured muscles would let her towards her medical trailer. Work. That was what she needed. Something to keep her busy and stop her from thinking.

'Okay, everyone,' Philip called from his position high above one of the mobile cameras, 'take your positions, please. Let's roll.'

Elizabeth settled in one of the camp chairs close by. She had finished her clinic. As usual there had been little for her to do except dole out some antibiotics and painkillers. This job was fine for the time being but once she was finished here she'd have to think seriously about which direction she wanted her career to go in. If she was honest, she missed the rush of emergency medicine. She also knew that she had been in no state to go back to that speciality straight after Charlie's death. At least now she was beginning to think about the future.

She turned her attention to what was happening on set.

Kendrick was made up to look like Jack while Josh was dressed to look like one of the baddies, and some of the other crew members had been drafted in as extras. Imogen was wearing a red wig to make her look like Tara.

The fight was taking place inside the mock-up of one of the buildings and everyone moved inside. The set had been made to look like a restaurant. Elizabeth had been given the script by one of the assistants and she found the scene. Apparently the hero—or Kendrick, in this instance—was to be set on by ten or so villains. He would fight his way out of trouble with his fists and in the middle there was a bit where he would leap from the balcony onto the shoulders of one of the baddies—in this case Josh—before ending up victorious.

Or so it was scripted.

A pile of cardboard boxes was being piled up at the foot of the balcony by Kendrick's team.

He would have to fall just right so he didn't hurt himself.

The fight was so realistic that Elizabeth found herself sucking in a breath every time Kendrick took a blow.

At one point Kendrick jumped over the balcony and onto Josh's back. The next moment he and Josh were rolling around on the floor as if they were genuinely involved in a fight to the death. When Josh's fist actually connected with Kendrick's jaw, Elizabeth winced. That had to have hurt.

'Cut. Okay, folks, that's a wrap,' Philip called. 'Good job, everyone.'

Kendrick helped Josh to his feet. Elizabeth noticed a cut on Kendrick's forehead that was bleeding badly. She was on her feet in an instant, stopping only to reach for her medical bag.

'You're hurt. Let me take a look,' she said.

Kendrick reached a hand towards his head and seemed surprised when it came away sticky with blood. 'Hey, Josh, did you do this?' he said. 'I thought I'd trained you better.'

'You've got to be kidding me,' Josh retorted. 'If I'd connected with you, you would have known all about it. You must have hit your head on something.'

'It doesn't matter how you got it,' Elizabeth said. 'I need to clean you up.'

She slipped on a pair of sterile gloves. 'Come and sit down under the light so I can see it better.'

With a wink at Josh, Kendrick let himself be led over to a chair. Elizabeth angled the light so she could see better. Thankfully the wound wasn't deep enough to require stitches. There was also a bruise coming up on Kendrick's cheekbone.

'I'll clean the cut and apply some Steri-strips. I've got some arnica in my bag that I can put on the bruise. That should help.'

Kendrick leaned back in his chair and as Elizabeth bent to clean his head wound she was uncomfortably aware of his breath on her neck. She hoped to hell he wouldn't notice it was giving her goose-bumps.

'Take your time, Doc,' Kendrick drawled.

Kendrick leaned back, enjoying the feel of her cool fingers on his head. Normally he'd have cleaned it up himself and just stuck a sticky plaster on but he was enjoying this way too much to want to stop Elizabeth from doing whatever she was doing. The touch of her fingers made his gut clench.

Her perfume drifted across, intoxicating him, and when she bent over he could see the swell of her breasts just above the open button of her shirt.

What he wouldn't do to feel that soft, pale skin under his fingertips. To thread his hands through her thick hair, to take away that guarded expression from her eyes.

And he would. It was only a matter of time.

She had finished applying the makeshift stitches to his forehead and was pressing lightly on his bruised cheek.

He swallowed a groan.

Before he could stop himself he took her hand and held it away from his face.

'If you carry on doing that, I won't be responsible for my actions,' he growled. 'I'm only human.'

'Don't be ridiculous,' she replied, but not before he saw the answering spark in her eyes. Perhaps the ice maiden was starting to thaw. Maybe on the next stunt he could really hurt himself. He was damned if he didn't want to see the look of concern in her eyes again.

CHAPTER FIVE

IN THE end the decision whether to go to Los Angeles was taken out of Elizabeth's hands when Philip announced late on Thursday evening that he'd decided to film a scene in the city.

The cast and crew drove down in convoy, leaving when it was still dark the next morning. Kendrick had offered to take Elizabeth on his motorbike, but she had refused politely. The thought of spending a couple of hours with her arms wrapped around his waist was unnerving. He hadn't said anything but his mocking eyes had suggested he knew exactly why she'd opted to travel with the crew.

They drove into LA and along Sunset Boulevard, with its giant boards advertising the latest movies, just as it was getting light.

The next part of the filming would take place in a studio on the outskirts of the city.

The stunt for the interior scene didn't involve

Kendrick. The female stuntwoman, Imogen, who was doubling for Tara, had to fall down a flight of steps. Elizabeth thought they would use all sorts of equipment to mimic the fall and was surprised when Imogen stood at the top of the stairs dressed as Tara's character without any pulleys, wires or padding. Imogen was wearing the red wig again and from where Elizabeth was standing looked pretty much like the star. Kendrick had explained that while they tried to get doubles for the stunt that were close in appearance to the stars, make-up and wigs usually had to be added.

'It's not as if the camera gets a close-up of the doubles,' he'd said. 'We learn to keep our faces away from the camera. The success of the stunt depends on the audience believing that it really is the actor.'

Kendrick and Imogen had spent the last half an hour with Philip, discussing what the stunt-woman would do and where the cameras should be positioned in order to get the best shot.

'Okay, we're hot.'

'Everyone get clear.'

On command, Imogen pretended to fall down the stairs. She tumbled down, making no attempt to shield herself as her body bounced from wall to wall.

Elizabeth was shocked. She could break her neck. And as Imogen lay at the bottom of the steps, not moving, she thought her worst fears had been realised and started to move towards her. Forget Philip and his insistence she stay out of the shot until he gave the all-clear. She was here to make sure her charges stayed alive and no director, no matter how much of a Hollywood big shot he might be, was going to make her do otherwise.

But even as she was running towards Imogen, Philip was calling 'Cut' and the stuntwoman was getting into a sitting position, rubbing her wrist.

Before Elizabeth could reach her, Kendrick had got there first and was talking to his colleague.

Imogen brushed herself off and stood up.

'Did you hurt your wrist?' Elizabeth asked. 'Can I have a look?'

'It's nothing,' Imogen said dismissively. 'You want me to do it again, boss?'

When Kendrick nodded, Elizabeth couldn't believe what she was hearing.

She took Imogen by the upper arm and studied

her wrist. It was already beginning to swell. Probably a bad sprain, but she should get it X-rayed to be on the safe side.

'I'm afraid no more stunts for you today. At the very least you need to get that X-rayed.'

Imogen winked at Kendrick.

'Tell her, boss,' she said.

'It's not broken. She can do it again,' Kendrick said.

Elizabeth felt the slow burn of anger travel to her chest.

'May I remind you that I am the doctor? You may have experience—first-aid experience—in the army, but there's no way you are competent to make that diagnosis. I'm forbidding Imogen to do that scene, or any other scene, until I'm satisfied that her wrist isn't broken.'

Before she knew it, Kendrick was hustling her away from Imogen. She tried to struggle out of his grasp but his grip was too strong. He waited until they were out of earshot of the others.

She rounded on him furiously. How dared he treat her like some sort of…? She couldn't think of the right word. She was too angry.

'What the hell do you think you're doing? How

dare you manhandle me? How dare you drag me away from my patient?'

'How sure are you that Immy's wrist is broken?' Kendrick remained implacable in the face of her fury.

'I don't think it is, but I can't know for certain. Any responsible doctor would insist on an X-ray.'

'If Immy doesn't think it's broken then it's not. Believe me, she's had enough experience of being injured to know.' He dropped his voice. 'Stuntmen and women get paid by the gag they do. If you take her off the set now, just to satisfy your own need for reassurance, she'll lose money.'

Elizabeth glared at him.

'Hey, Kendrick, we need to get on,' Philip shouted across. 'Can't you two leave any discussion for later?'

'I'm not going to let her do it again,' Elizabeth said. 'It's my decision.'

Kendrick looked at her for one long moment. Clearly he wasn't used to being told what he could and couldn't do. Then his face relaxed. 'You are one stubborn woman. Tell you what, I'll ask Josh if he'll do the stunt. I'd do it myself except I'm too tall to pass for Tara. I suspect Josh won't be too happy about dressing up as a woman but, hey, I owe him for that punch he landed on me. Will that keep you happy?'

He was putting her in a difficult position. If Josh hurt himself, she would feel responsible. She opened her mouth to protest but he cut her off.

'Lizzie, I'm not asking you. I'm telling you.' Now it was his turn to frown at her.

Kendrick turned away and, after a quick word with Philip, Imogen left the set. Philip was drumming his fingers on the camera. 'Can we get on, please? Will someone tell the doctor that she's not here to get in the way of filming?'

A flash of annoyance passed across Kendrick's face and he turned to Philip. 'If the doc says someone's not fit to do a stunt then we listen. Josh is going to do it instead.'

There was a moment when Philip and Kendrick faced each other, before Philip sighed loudly. 'Could you at least make it quick?'

A small smile crossed Kendrick's face. 'I just need five minutes to persuade him and get him into the right clothes.'

As Kendrick turned away he winked at Elizabeth and she glared back. She didn't want him running interference for her. She was perfectly able to stand up for herself.

'It's going to take time to get Josh organised.' Philip's look at Elizabeth left her in no doubt he held her responsible for the delay but she held her head high. What use was she to anyone if she let them push her around? She would rather pack her bags and leave than go against her professional judgement. Not that she wanted to leave, she realised with an unpleasant sinking feeling in her stomach. She liked it here. The last thing she needed or wanted right now was to be looking for a new job.

'Let's do the scene with Jack and Tara in the meantime,' Philip continued, with a last baleful look at Elizabeth.

Tough. They could all glare at her as much as they liked. It wouldn't change her mind. She crossed over to where Imogen was sitting, flexing her arm. From the movement Elizabeth knew it couldn't be broken. Still, she wanted to get it strapped. In her peripheral vision she could see Kendrick and Josh talking. From the heated look on Josh's face he wasn't too happy at having to stand in for Imogen. However, after a final word from Kendrick, Josh turned on his heel and stomped off towards the dressing area.

Elizabeth turned her attention to the injured stuntwoman. 'Hey, Imogen, you okay with me strapping your wrist?'

Imogen looked at her with a look of admiration. 'You did a brave thing back there. We don't usually see the medical support standing up to Philip. The only one who usually gets away with it is Kendrick. Philip knows he needs him, and us, to make the film look good.'

Elizabeth called to one of the production assistants for some ice. 'Keep your arm high and we'll put this ice pack on. It should alleviate most of the swelling. After that I'll strap it and if it looks okay, you might be all right for tomorrow's filming.'

'Sure hope so. We're doing some car-chase scenes and I need my wrist to be working. But I should tell you that this little bump is nothing compared to what I've worked through before. You'll find out that most of us carry on unless we're laid up in hospital. It's the nature of the job.'

When Elizabeth was satisfied that Imogen's wrist had been sufficiently iced, she took a bandage out of her medical bag and deftly strapped her affected limb. In the meantime, an unhappy-looking Josh, wearing a dress and red wig, strode back onto the set. Elizabeth and Imogen shared a smile.

'Ready when you are, Philip,' Kendrick called over. 'How's it going, Immy? That's a pretty neat bandage you have there.'

'The doc insisted,' Imogen replied. 'I did try to tell her it was nothing but a little bump, but she wouldn't listen.' She looked from Kendrick to Elizabeth. 'I suspect our doc isn't used to being told what to do any more than you are. That should make it interesting around here for the next few weeks.'

Elizabeth started. What did Imogen mean? Had she picked up on the tension between Kendrick and herself whenever they were together?

'I feel ridiculous in this get-up,' Josh complained. 'Maybe we should have got the doc to stand in for Immy.' He winked at Elizabeth to let her know there were no bad feelings. 'But can we get this over and done with so I can get back to being a man?'

Everyone laughed and Kendrick punched Josh

lightly on the shoulder. 'I guess you'd better go and fall down some stairs to keep Philip happy. I'll watch it on camera. Make a good job of it and you won't have to do it again.'

Josh's fall was a repeat of Imogen's. Fortunately he seemed to survive his tumble unscathed. Nevertheless, it took another couple of attempts before Kendrick declared himself satisfied with the take.

'Okay, that's a wrap,' Philip called, after Kendrick and his team had huddled around the camera, checking that they were satisfied with the shot. Elizabeth had noticed that it seemed to be as much to do with Kendrick as Philip when it came to deciding whether a stunt was good enough not to require repeating.

'I need everyone back on set on Sunday lunchtime at the latest. I guess I'll see most of you tonight.'

As cast and crew began to disperse, Kendrick walked across to Elizabeth.

'How about I show you around?' Kendrick asked. 'I'm assuming you don't want to spend the rest of the day back at your hotel.'

'I'd planned to go and see Sunny at the hospital this afternoon.'

'So did I, so I checked with Sunny earlier. She asked if we could come for the afternoon visiting. Something about her having more than her quota for this morning.'

'In that case, I do have the morning free.'

'I could use one of the company's helicopters and take you up the coast,' Kendrick suggested.

Elizabeth gave a mock shudder. 'I'd really prefer something a little less exciting.'

Kendrick gave her a lopsided grin and clasped a hand to his chest. 'Hey, are you saying you don't trust me? I'm a pretty good pilot, you know.' He paused. 'I know a great restaurant overlooking the Big Sur. We could go there for lunch and then go for a walk on the beach.'

That sounded too much like a date.

'Maybe another time? I wouldn't mind just going for a walk and having a look around. I've always wanted to see Venice Beach.'

'Sounds good to me. I'll meet you outside in five minutes,' Kendrick said. 'I just need to change into something more modern.'

Venice Beach was a place Elizabeth had heard about but never seen. The strange but pleasing thing about Los Angeles was that everything was exactly like how it was depicted in the movies. She was beginning to see how some people might feel that they were living on a film set. There were beautiful women in shorts and crop tops roller-skating and Elizabeth couldn't help but notice that Kendrick's eyes were swivelling as they walked. A little further on was Muscle Beach. This time it was Elizabeth's turn to gawp at the bare-chested men lifting weights and lapping up the attention of the bystanders.

Along one side was a range of shops advertising the services of spiritual healers and psychics. There were even places offering therapy for pets. It made her smile. Only in California…

Leaving the promenade, they strolled onto the beach. The sun was high in a cloudless sky. Elizabeth slipped off her shoes, enjoying the sensation of sand between her toes. Neither said anything about their earlier difference of opinion. Elizabeth was sure Kendrick wasn't a man to harbour a grudge.

As they walked, several of the bikini-clad wannabe starlets who were parading their toned and tanned bodies gave Kendrick interested looks. He seemed oblivious to their unabashed admiration. Elizabeth could have sworn that Kendrick wasn't the type to pass up the opportunity to flirt. On the other hand, he was probably used to female attention.

'Do you have a girlfriend?' Elizabeth asked. The words were out before she could stop them. Great, he was bound to make some smart remark about why she wanted to know.

But to her surprise, instead of the usual flashing smile, a shadow crossed Kendrick's face. 'No,' he said quietly. 'Not any more.'

'Not any more' was an odd way to put it. Why not say 'Not at the moment'?

Once more she had the feeling that there was more to Kendrick than his easygoing exterior.

'Ever been married?'

'No, and not likely to be,' he said.

Elizabeth could have sworn something shifted behind his eyes. She had clearly touched a nerve. Perhaps he wasn't quite as tough as he liked to pretend? She had the distinct impression that there had been someone and the relationship hadn't ended well. But she valued her own privacy too highly not to respect his. If he wanted to tell her, he would. Nevertheless, she was intensely curious. She suspected that despite his playboy exterior Kendrick wasn't a man who gave his heart lightly.

'Are you ready for something to eat?' Kendrick asked.

'Sure. Where do you suggest? There appears to be a million restaurants and cafés.'

'I know just the place. I have a cabin along at Malibu. It's only a little further along the coast. It's quieter. We could pick up a sandwich and something to drink from one of the delis and have it on the beach.'

Elizabeth's heart kicked against her ribs. What was he asking? She was about to refuse when he turned his deep blue eyes on her.

'I need to pick up something from there to give to Josh.'

She hesitated for the briefest moment then gave herself a mental shake. As Kendrick had said, it would only take a few minutes and she found herself intensely curious to see where he lived.

'Lead the way,' she said with a smile.

'So this is where you live?' Elizabeth said, surprised. Whatever else she had expected, it hadn't been this small cabin perched on the edge of the beach. On the other hand, it was exactly where Kendrick would live. He would never do the conventional.

'It belonged to my folks, way back when they got married. Before this part became fashionable. I bought it off them as soon as I was earning money.'

He took Elizabeth by the hand and pulled her up the wooden steps and onto the deck.

'It's so, so…cute. I love it.' The small cabin was painted white with a picket fence and a deck overlooking the beach, which was only a short walk away.

'Cute?' Kendrick pulled a face. 'I don't want to live in a house that anyone calls cute.'

'Doesn't quite go with your image? Then I guess you shouldn't have painted that adorable picket fence. You should have put up a steel fence— all barbed wire and spiky. Would that have been better? More in keeping with the owner?'

Kendrick grinned at her, a deep dimple appearing in each cheek. On any other man this might have made him look feminine. On Kendrick, however, it had the effect of making him look ten times sexier. As if he wasn't sexy enough.

The air between them fizzed. Elizabeth could have sworn every hair on her body was standing up. Maybe it hadn't been a good idea to come here after all.

She must have been staring because he winked at her. She didn't want his swollen head getting any bigger.

'It must be worth a fortune,' she said, simply to say something.

Kendrick pretended to look shocked. 'Didn't think you were the type of woman who cared too much about that kind of stuff. Don't tell me I've got you all wrong, Dr Morgan.'

'Oh, I'm as venial as any other woman.' She grinned back at him. 'I need to be kept in shoes at the very least.'

Damn! That could definitely be construed as flirting, and Kendrick didn't need any encouragement.

'Can I see inside?' she said quietly. She was dying to look for more clues about this man.

'Help yourself, but there's not much to see.'

To an extent he was right. Along one complete

wall of the sitting room were a number of surf-boards propped up against the wall. On the other side were what seemed like sails for a windsurfer and still more equipment. The absolute minimum amount of space was left for a couple of arm-chairs that had seen better days and a TV. Clearly Kendrick wasn't home a great deal.

'You surf?' she asked, pointing to the boards.

'Whenever I can. Don't always get the right waves here, though. Sometimes I meet up with my cousin, Fabio, and go in search of the big ones.'

'What else? Windsurfing, by the look of this stuff.' She indicated the other side of the room with a sweep of her hand.

'Kite-surfing. You use a kite as well as a surf-board. It lets you do tricks. I could teach you if you like.'

Elizabeth shook her head. 'Oh, no, you don't. You've already almost got me killed once.'

Kendrick drew his eyebrows together. 'Almost got you killed? When?'

'When you took me out on the horse.'

He threw his head back and laughed. 'Believe me, you were in no real danger.' His expression grew serious. 'I would never let anything happen to you.'

The way he was looking at her was making her bones feel as if they were melting. She gave herself a little shake. She needed to remember Kendrick could no more not flirt than she could, what? Not be a doctor?

But it was as if there was a magnetic field surrounding him that drew her to him and her brain was sending wild thoughts to her heart. In this man's arms she could forget.

He hooked his fingers into the waistband of her jeans and pulled her into him.

She raised her head, meeting his eyes. They were as cool as the sea after the rain, and just as fathomless. Fathomless but she could tell that he wanted her. He looked at her for one long moment as her head continued to spin and she was powerless to stop him. She didn't want to stop him. Although her head was screaming that she should, her body seemed to have developed a mind of its own.

He brought his mouth down on hers. His lips were warm, soft and hard at the same time. His hands grasped her hips and pulled her even closer.

His mouth on hers was like an electric shock. Her body sparked and a liquid warmth spread through her as she moulded her body to his.

His hands were plucking her shirt from the waistband of her jeans, the rough skin of his fingers on her back before his hands moved across her stomach, lightly, gently, feeling her skin, his mouth never leaving hers.

She heard a moan come from somewhere and realised with a shock that it had come from her.

He lifted his head and his eyes glittered down at her.

It was enough. She pulled away, conscious that her breath was coming in little gasps and all too conscious that her body was screaming out to be touched again.

'No, Kendrick. Please. I can't.' She was aware the words were coming out in little, breathless gasps.

'Why not?' he said easily, reaching for her again.

She moved away from him, putting as much distance between them as possible. If she let him touch her again, she'd never be able to tell him to stop. Although she wanted the oblivion being in his arms would bring, it would be temporary.

Giving in to him would lead to complications she didn't need.

'I just can't.'

The look he gave her was inscrutable. 'I would never force anyone. One day you'll want me as much as I want you. I can wait for then.'

His arrogance was breathtaking. But, then, hadn't she kissed him back with a passion that she'd never experienced before?

'I wouldn't hold my breath if I were you,' she said. 'Some women can resist you, you know. Women who have a bit of pride. Women like me.'

She made a show of looking at her watch. 'Isn't it time we headed to the hospital?'

The good thing about being behind Kendrick on his Harley-Davidson was that it made conversation impossible. The bad thing was that the feel of his body under her hands was doing nothing to calm her overheated libido. She was relieved when they pulled up outside the hospital and there was some distance between her and Kendrick once again.

Inside her private room, Sunny was sitting

up in bed. Despite her pallor, she was clearly on the mend.

'The doctors say if you hadn't spotted that I had malaria when you did, it could have been really serious. Thank you both.'

'I think you have to thank Kendrick,' Elizabeth demurred. 'Without him, it would have taken another day or two for me to arrive at a diagnosis.'

Sunny raised her face to let Kendrick kiss her cheek. 'He's a bit of a dark horse our Kendrick, isn't he?'

Just then two children scampered into the room and Sunny held open her arms as they flung themselves on top of her.

'Hey, sweeties. Did you miss Mummy last night?'

Elizabeth felt a stab of pain so sharp it took her breath away. She would have given her life to be able to hold her daughter like Sunny was holding hers. Trixie was six. What would Charlie have been like had she lived? What would she have been like at six? At eighteen? As a mother? What would the future have held for her child?

It was pointless to torment herself like that. Turning away so no one would see the tears that burned behind her eyelids, she arranged the flowers she had brought in a vase one of the nurses had provided. When she swung around a few minutes later, it was to find Kendrick watching her speculatively. She got the impression that he didn't miss much.

'We should leave you to spend time with your family,' he told Sunny. 'We just wanted to say hello.'

'Thanks for taking the time, guys. But don't worry 'bout me. At least this way I get to spend time with these two,' Sunny said, hugging her children close. 'Although the doctors think I'll be able to come back to work next week, so I'll see you both then. As long as you promise to tell me all about the party the next time I see you.'

They left Sunny cuddling her children. When they were out of hearing range, Kendrick took Elizabeth by the shoulder and gently turned her so that she was facing him.

'What's wrong?' he asked. 'Back there, something upset you. Do you want to tell me what it was?'

Elizabeth forced herself to hold his gaze.

'There's nothing to tell. I'm just glad to see that Sunny is doing okay.'

She could tell that Kendrick didn't believe her. He looked at her intently for a moment but said nothing more.

'I'm fine, really,' she said again. But she wasn't—not really. 'I think I'll take a cab back to the hotel. I'm feeling a little bushed.'

'Forget the cab, I'll take you.'

Elizabeth panicked. She needed time on her own. Away from Kendrick's searching looks. Time to regain her composure. 'I'd much rather take a cab. You don't have to keep watching out for me, you know.' But didn't a small secret part of her like it that he did? It had been a long time since she'd been able to share her problems. She gave herself a mental shake. Her head was all over the place. She had to get away from him.

Kendrick frowned. 'Are you sure you're feeling okay? You don't look that great to me.'

'I promise you I'm fine,' Elizabeth said with as much conviction as she could muster. In some ways the flirting, teasing Kendrick was easier to deal with than the one who looked at her as if he could see into her head. If he was kind to her, she didn't know if she could stop herself from throwing herself into his arms and sharing her pain.

He let her arm drop. 'It's probably not a bad idea to get some rest before tonight.' His teasing smile was back. 'Jack's parties have quite a reputation. They often go on way into the next day.'

Elizabeth forced a smile. 'I'll look forward to it. In the meantime, I'm sure you have things you'd like to be getting on with.'

As soon as the cab dropped her outside her hotel, she hurried up to her room. Inside she leaned against the door, and the tears she'd been holding back came in deep painful sobs. Just when she had thought she was coping, something would happen: the simple sight of a mother holding her two healthy children had brought her carefully held-together veneer crashing down. Back there at the hospital, she'd been shocked at the raw jealousy she'd felt when she'd seen Sunny with her two children. She slid to the floor and buried her face in her hands.

'Oh, Charlie. When is it going to stop hurting like this?'

By the time the tears had stopped, night had fallen. She hadn't cried like that since Charlie's funeral and in an odd way it felt good. A quick glance at her watch told her that she had half an hour to get ready for the party.

Jack had insisted on sending a driver and limousine to pick her up at the hotel. She hadn't thought to pack a party dress, so black jeans, a glitzy belt and a silk blouse would have to do. After her shower, Elizabeth sat down at the dressing table, putting on her make-up. When was the last time she'd done this? It was hard to remember.

Her thoughts returned to the kiss she'd shared with Kendrick. She couldn't remember ever being kissed like that. The touch of his lips on hers had turned her into a quivering wreck. And that had just been a kiss. What would it be like to be loved by him? She shook her head. It was crazy to let her thoughts go in that direction. Hadn't she told herself over and over that getting involved with Kendrick wasn't an option? Given the state her heart was in, it was far too dangerous. But back then when he'd kissed her, the world had stopped and the darkness in her soul had disappeared. It had only lasted while she'd been in his arms, but she had to admit it had felt good to forget, if only for a little while.

Clipping on gold earrings, she surveyed her image with a critical eye. The hot Californian sun had dusted her skin with a light tan and highlighted her hair. At least she looked healthier than the washed-out, exhausted shadow of a woman of a couple of weeks ago. She looked like a woman who could be happy. The thought brought her up short. Slowly she unclipped her earrings and dropped them back onto her dressing table. Apart from having to face Kendrick, did she really want to spend the night talking to complete strangers? Maybe another time, but tonight at least she was better on her own. When Jack's driver came for her, she would tell him she'd changed her mind.

Kendrick tossed the keys of his motorbike to a waiting valet. Set high up in Beverly Hills, the driveway of Jack's multimillion-dollar mansion was lined with sports cars. Kendrick scooped a glass of champagne from the tray of a passing waiter before heading into the house. The party must have started some time ago as it was in full swing. He scanned the crowd, searching for Lizzie, but she wasn't to be seen amongst the guests.

Nodding greetings to actors he knew, Kendrick weaved his way onto the wide veranda that circled the house. Models with barely-there bikinis and young men who looked as if they spent every minute in the gym posed around the infinity pool, hoping to be spotted by Philip or one of the other directors who would be at the party.

Kendrick was looking forward to seeing what Elizabeth would make of all this. He had the feeling she wouldn't be fazed in the slightest and would have some amusing comments to make.

Despite the fact she'd pulled away earlier at the cabin, he was making progress. No woman would kiss a man like she had if she didn't feel something. She was definitely thawing.

But the memory of her face back at the hospital kind of spoilt the satisfaction he was feeling. For once she'd let down her guard and he'd recognised something in her eyes that had shocked him. He'd seen that look staring back at him in the mirror after Amy had died.

Deep in thought, he wasn't aware of someone coming to stand behind him until two slender arms slid around his waist.

'Aren't you gonna ask me to dance, Kendrick?'

He was dismayed at the thudding disappointment he felt when he realised the voice didn't belong to Elizabeth. He unwrapped the arms from around his waist and turned towards the heavily made-up woman standing behind him. He would take Elizabeth's natural beauty any time.

'Hello…' What was her name again? Fiffy? Foofy? Something that sounded like a poodle's name at any rate.

'It's Fiffy. Don't tell me you've forgotten me already?' Fiffy pouted, trailing a manicured nail down the open neck of his shirt.

Something had upset Elizabeth back at the hospital. What was up with her?

'We could have a swim. Or a dance.' Fiffy entwined his arm in hers. 'Or we could go to your place.' Fiffy's plaintive voice brought him back to the present.

How did Fiffy know about his cabin? He made it a rule not to take anyone there. Until Elizabeth, that was.

A month ago, he would have taken up the invitation in Fiffy's eyes like a shot, but that had been before…before his head had become filled with thoughts of Elizabeth Morgan.

'Fiffy,' he said quietly, 'I can't get you a part in a movie. I've explained that before. And I mean it.'

Fiffy's eyes flashed with annoyance and Kendrick sighed. No matter how beautiful and desirable the woman, anything less than honest, mutually satisfying sex wasn't for him. He had always been completely upfront about that. These parties were losing their appeal. Maybe he had been to too many of them.

Kendrick grabbed Jack as he passed. 'Have you seen Lizzie?'

'She's not coming,' Jack said. 'Something about a headache.'

Kendrick turned back to the starlet. 'Fiffy, I really have to go. I'm happy to put a word in with Philip for you.' Without waiting for a reply, he walked away. He needed to find Lizzie and check that she was okay.

Elizabeth knew she'd made the right decision not to go to the party. It wasn't as if she would be missed. Seeing Sunny's kids today had shaken her to the core. There was no way she would have been up to making small talk.

She was interrupted from her musing by the roar of a motorbike and a part of her was unsurprised to see Kendrick pulling up outside. Instinctively she wrapped her arms around her body. She was only wearing pyjama bottoms and a T-shirt as she'd planned to go to bed soon.

'Kendrick!' She stood up and leaned over her first-floor balcony. 'What are you doing here? Is anything wrong? Does someone need me?'

'No, everything's fine. I came to see if *you* were okay.'

'Okay with me? Why shouldn't it be?'

'Look, Lizzie. Can I come up? I'm beginning to feel like Romeo to your Juliet down here.'

Elizabeth laughed, and some of the sadness lifted from her heart.

Truth was, she was glad to see him. She'd had enough of her own thoughts.

'I'll open the door for you.'

But before she had a chance, Kendrick had jumped onto the side railings of the veranda below and with a leap that belied his size grabbed her railings and swung himself onto her balcony.

'Can't you use the door like everyone else?' She smiled.

Kendrick shook his head. 'Nope. Not while there's an opportunity to impress a lady. You were impressed, weren't you?' he asked in mock dismay.

Elizabeth had to laugh. It felt good. And it felt even better that Kendrick was there.

She caught his eye and her breath froze in her throat.

Every instinct in Kendrick's body was telling him that he should leave this woman well alone, but yet he couldn't pull away from her. His heart was pounding as she looked up at him with luminous eyes.

He placed his hands on either side of her neck, letting his thumbs rest just under her jaw. Very gently he raised her face until her mouth was inches from his. Her eyes were dreamy, half-closed, but he could see in the dilation of her pupils that she wanted him too. And that was all it took.

He bent his head and found her mouth, tasting the sweetness and running his tongue over the softness of her lips. Taking his time, he explored her mouth with his tongue, increasing the pressure until she gasped and began kissing him back with a hunger that surprised but delighted him. Her body was pressed into his, and he dropped his hands to her hips to pull her closer. The last coherent thought he had as they tumbled onto her bed was that she wasn't an ice maiden after all.

Elizabeth lay with her head on Kendrick's chest, listening to the beat of his heart. Judging by the matching slow, steady rhythm of his breathing he had fallen asleep. Why did men always do that after making love? She, on the other hand, could have jumped out of bed, and...whatever. Not that she wanted to leave Kendrick's arms. It felt too good. Even while she knew it was a mistake.

But had it been? Kendrick wasn't Simon. And if he didn't want a relationship, neither did she. She was here for another month and after that who knew? She and Kendrick would go their separate ways. Why shouldn't she find some peace in this man's arms, if only for a little while? It wasn't as if she was planning to fall in love with him.

But haven't you already? a voice inside her whispered. *Even just a little bit?*

The voice was wrong. Dead wrong. She was attracted to Kendrick—sure. She found him unbelievably sexy, but part of what attracted her was the firm knowledge that whatever there was between them wasn't meant to last.

She traced the bullet hole on his shoulder with a fingertip and let her hand trail over the defined muscles of his chest, before trailing her hand down to where she could feel every muscle of his hard abdomen.

He groaned as she moved her hand lower still, exploring the ridges and contours of his body.

Suddenly he flipped her on her back and was staring down at her with glinting blue eyes.

He raised her hands above her head and pinned them there with one of his own.

'Do you trust me?' he asked huskily.

Her mouth was too dry to speak so she simply nodded.

'Then I want you to lie there and not move. Not a muscle. I want to kiss every inch of you slowly and watch your face while I do that.'

As he kissed her throat behind her ears, his lips moving slowly, inexorably downwards, her heart was thumping so hard against her ribs she thought it might just stop.

His mouth was on her breasts, taking each nipple in his mouth by turn, and she arched her back, wanting him. He stopped what he was doing for a second and looked at her, his eyes triumphant. 'You think that feels good? I haven't even started yet.'

Later, dressed once more—if you could call it that—in panties and her T-shirt, she sat between his long jeans-clad legs and leaned against his bare chest, nibbling on the cold lobster he had brought with him from the party. She had grabbed a blanket from the bed and laid it on the wooden balcony. He wrapped his arms about her, keeping her close. The night was warm, with just the merest hint of a breeze, and the sky was studded with stars.

The crickets chirped in the distance and somewhere an owl hooted.

'I never thought I'd end up in bed with you,' she said.

'I knew we would,' he replied.

'Sure of yourself, aren't you?' She knew she should have been angry or offended or something, but she wasn't. She liked his honesty. She couldn't have borne it if he'd lied to her. All she wanted from him was this simple, direct and honest need for each other.

* * *

As daylight seeped through the window of her hotel, Elizabeth slipped out of bed and pulled her oversized T-shirt over her head. Kendrick was still sleeping. He slept as he did everything—with utter abandon. He lay on his back with his arms flung over his head and the sheet tangled between his thighs. Thinking about his thighs made the heat rise in Elizabeth's face. Their love-making had been everything it had never been with Simon. Passionate, caring and adventurous. Was she doing the right thing, getting involved with Kendrick? If she hadn't needed to be comforted, would she have slept with him? But it hadn't been just comfort, she had to admit. In his arms she had felt alive for the first time since Charlie had died.

Kendrick stirred in his sleep and frowned. Could it be that his dreams were as haunted as hers? Elizabeth realised with a jolt that last night, wrapped in his arms, had been the first time she hadn't dreamt of Charlie. Although she would never see Kendrick once she had left here, he was helping her to heal inside and she couldn't regret that.

His eyes flickered and immediately he was alert. He sat up in bed and grinned at her. 'Hey,' he said softly, reaching an arm towards her, 'why don't you come over here?'

Elizabeth wrapped her arms around her body. 'What is this, Kendrick?'

He tossed the tangled sheets aside and came to stand in front of her. His nakedness was doing all sorts of crazy things to her insides.

'It's what we want it to be. Two people enjoying being with each other.'

'Because you have to know I'll never get married again,' she blurted, then felt such an idiot. No one had mentioned marriage. She didn't even know if they had a future beyond last night.

'Who said anything about getting married?' The air seemed to cool between them. 'I was being honest when I said that marriage wasn't on the cards. If I misled you, I'm sorry.'

'I know you did and I know you meant it, but so do I. I don't even think this was a good idea.' She swept out her arm, taking in the crumpled bedclothes.

The corners of his eyes creased. With his tousled hair and the heat in his eyes he had never seemed so sexy or so dangerous. 'I think it's a very good idea. You said last night you didn't want to think about the past or the future, and neither do I. Why don't we see what each day brings? No promises on either side. It seems to me as if you need some lightness in your life and, for the record, so do I.' He pulled her closer and his hands were on her hips underneath her T-shirt. As he ran his hands across her bottom and up across the small of her back she melted into him.

CHAPTER SIX

ELIZABETH clutched Kendrick's waist as if her life depended on it, and maybe it did. Who did he think he was now? Not that it mattered, she thought, suppressing a scream as they tore around another corner, the bike leaning so far it was almost caressing the tarmac.

She yelped as they passed between two cars. Kendrick was so carefree and full of life it was liberating.

The realisation hit her like a ton of bricks. Since Charlie had died, hadn't a part of her longed to be with her daughter? Wasn't that why she'd run, taking this job, knowing if she stayed a moment longer in the home that reminded her of Charlie she would drown in her grief? Now she knew without a shadow of doubt that she wanted to live. Even if the future still seemed bleak.

They were behind a bus now. It was probably heading towards Palm Desert, as they were.

Elizabeth was about to yell in Kendrick's ear that he should slow down when all of a sudden there was an almighty bang and the coach weaved from side to side.

Kendrick braked sharply and only managed to miss the out-of-control bus by a whisker.

As he brought the bike to a halt at the roadside, the sound of screeching metal increased until the air was filled with it. Horrified, Elizabeth watched as almost in slow motion the bus tipped onto its side. For a second she thought it was going to right itself, but it was too late. The weight of the bus was already too much on the left and it was sliding on its side along the tarmac. Kendrick and Elizabeth were so close they could hear the screams from inside the bus.

There was a moment of shocked, eerie silence then she and Kendrick were off the bike and running towards the bus.

Kendrick was punching numbers into his phone as he ran.

'I've alerted the emergency services,' he called as he caught up with her. 'I've told them to send fire engines as well as Ambulances.

Elizabeth's heart was pounding so loud she could hardly hear him.

'We're going to have to triage them,' she said. 'Can you help me?'

'Don't worry,' he said grimly. 'I've done this before.'

Already some of the passengers were climbing from the wreckage, looking dazed.

'Please, sit down over there.' Elizabeth pointed to the roadside. 'Keep away from the road itself, and wait until either I or the emergency services gets to you.'

She was about to clamber through one of the open emergency windows when she felt a hand on her arm.

'I'll go first,' Kendrick said.

She shook his arm away. 'Kendrick. I'm the doctor. Those people inside need me.'

But he had already slipped past her and was disappearing inside the bus. Elizabeth followed.

It was difficult to see what was going on inside. The bus being on its side had tossed everyone sitting on the right over to the left and there was no way to tell how many injured lay under the mass of bodies.

Kendrick was systematically picking his way through the wreckage, stopping at each passenger and giving them a brief once-over, pointing those who could walk to the safety of the emergency exit. As he moved through the coach several more people struggled to their feet and Elizabeth helped them out.

'Lizzie. Over here!' Kendrick called her over.

She squeezed her way past the exiting passengers until she was next to him. He was bent over an elderly lady who was clutching her chest, clearly in shock.

Elizabeth felt for a pulse. It was more rapid than normal, but that was only to be expected, given the circumstances. As far as she could tell, the woman was in no immediate danger.

'My Bill,' the elderly woman gasped. 'Where is my Bill? He was sitting next to me.'

A glance at Kendrick told her he was thinking the same thing. Bill was very likely trapped underneath the twisted metal.

'What's your name, honey?' Kendrick asked.

'Martha. But please.' She clutched Kendrick's shirt. 'You have to find my Bill.'

'Take it easy, ma'am,' Kendrick said gently. 'I'll

find him, don't you worry. But first we're going to have to get you out of here. Do you think you can stand for me?'

While Kendrick was seeing to Martha, Elizabeth clambered back towards the front. She had to check the driver, although she doubted he would have stood a chance. And she was right. The driver was staring upwards, his neck at an unnatural angle, his unseeing eyes staring into space. Elizabeth leaned over him and gently closed his eyes before turning back to the rear of the bus. With most if not all the walking wounded having made their way out of the bus, only now would they be able to determine whether anyone was trapped and hurt—or, God help them, dead.

Kendrick squeezed past her, supporting Martha. As he passed he shook his head. Either Bill was dead or he couldn't find him.

Elizabeth stepped over the wreckage, stopping every foot or so to lift a piece of metal. She could hear Martha's cries for her husband coming from outside and Kendrick's voice, low and reassuring. If Bill was in here, she had to find him.

And then she saw it. A foot sticking out from

beneath tangled metal that must have been a seat at one time. Dropping to her knees, she called out to Kendrick, frantically trying to lift the twisted bits of steel. God, could anyone have survived underneath this?

She was almost crying with frustration when she felt Kendrick beside her. She was lifted and set aside.

'Let me,' Kendrick said. 'I'm stronger.'

Within a few minutes Kendrick had exposed Bill's head. Although there was a deep gash in the old man's forehead and he was deathly pale, he was still alive. She had to get better access to him. Suddenly she became aware of smoke and raised her head. Flames were licking at the back of the bus.

'Elizabeth, you need to get out of here. If the fire takes hold, the bus could explode.' Kendrick's voice was calm.

'I'm not going anywhere,' Elizabeth said. 'Not until Bill's okay.'

Kendrick held her stare and she saw something flash in his eyes. Incongruously he grinned. 'Then we'd better get Bill stabilised and hope that the fire service gets here soon.'

As Kendrick continued to pull the remains of the seat away, more and more of Bill came into view. Elizabeth felt along his legs and up across his torso. As far as she could tell, nothing was broken. That was good. But she couldn't tell how badly he'd injured his head or whether he'd hurt his neck. If they attempted to move him without supporting his neck, they could paralyse him. Damn. If she'd been driving her own car, she would have had a neck brace. It was no use thinking like that. She had nothing. Only her hands... and Kendrick.

Kendrick was removing his shirt and twisting it into a snake-like scarf. Immediately Elizabeth guessed what he was doing. As a makeshift neck brace, it wasn't prefect, but it could make the difference.

The flames were higher now and the interior of the bus was filling with smoke. If they didn't get Bill out, he could die from smoke inhalation. They all could. If fire didn't get them first.

'It's okay, Lizzie,' Kendrick said quietly. 'The bus runs on diesel. It's less likely to explode. But we should get out soon.'

She was easing the makeshift neck brace under Bill's neck.

'You go. I'll carry Bill.'

'It'll be safer if we lift him between the two of us.'

Kendrick looked as if he was about to protest, but he nodded as if he knew he'd be wasting time arguing with her. Crouching, he manoeuvred himself into the space behind Bill and placed his hands under his arms. When Kendrick gave her a sign to let her know they were ready, she took hold of Bill's legs and together they lifted the injured man. Inch by inch, aware that the flames were getting closer, they made their way along the bus to the open emergency exit.

Just as they were reaching the exit, the sound of sirens filled the air. Elizabeth's legs almost buckled with relief. Getting their patient out of the bus was a far trickier procedure than lifting him along the narrow corridor of the bus. They could wait here for the rescue team to arrive. There was enough fresh air for them to breathe and in the meantime she could monitor Bill's breathing.

Catching Kendrick's eyes, she knew he was thinking the same thing. He was in a more precarious position than she was. His escape route was blocked by Bill and her.

'I'm okay,' he said. 'Just do what you have to. They'll get us out in no time.'

Kendrick and Elizabeth watched as the last of the walking wounded were lifted into ambulances and taken to hospital to be checked over. The fire service trucks and police would remain at the accident scene until the bus had been towed away and the crash scene returned to normal. She looked down at her gold blouse, noting it was covered in blood from Bill's head wound.

As the adrenaline seeped away, Elizabeth started to shake.

Kendrick picked up his leather jacket from the ground and placed it over her shoulders.

'Are you okay?' he asked.

'I'm glad you were with me,' Elizabeth said. 'I don't know how I would have managed if you hadn't been here.' And it was true. Kendrick had been calm and methodical, as if he were used to dealing with multiple casualties every day.

'You would have coped.' He looked at her with admiration in his eyes. 'Bill owes his life to you.'

A silence stretched between them as their eyes locked. Why couldn't Simon have been more like this man? She couldn't imagine Kendrick deserting his wife and child when the going got tough. Despite his casual, laid-back manner there was something solid and dependable about Kendrick and despite the alarm bells going off in her head she remembered what it felt to be held in this man's arms. Safe, secure, but also dangerous. And dangerous was the part she had to remember. She shouldn't confuse his ability to cope in an emergency with dependability. She had no reason to think Kendrick was any different to Simon. But at least Kendrick wasn't making any promises.

'Come on, then,' Kendrick said, 'There's nothing more we can do here.'

As if he knew she had had enough excitement for one day, the journey back to the film set was taken at a much gentler speed. Tiredness washed over her and she leaned herself against his back, savouring the solid feel of him.

'I'm going to shower,' Kendrick said when they arrived back at the set, deserted except for the security personnel who waved them in with a nod and a smile of recognition. 'I suggest you do the same. Then I'll rustle us up something to eat.'

Elizabeth shook her head. 'I'm not hungry.' But then, as another wave of tiredness and dizziness washed over her, she swayed.

'Hey, hey, hey,' Kendrick said, and before she knew it she was being swept up into his arms.

She wriggled, but it was no use. Kendrick held her too firmly.

He kicked open the door of her trailer with his boot and pushed his way inside. He placed her gently on her sofa and turned towards her bathroom.

'Take off your clothes,' he said, 'while I turn on the shower. Then you're going to get into bed while I organise us some food. You should have something.'

'I'm okay,' Elizabeth mumbled, too tired to protest. 'Perfectly able to get myself showered. I might have a little nap first.'

Reaching behind the bathroom door, he found her robe and tossed it to her.

'If you don't remove those clothes, I'll do it for you.'

The tone of his voice left her in no doubt he

meant what he said. She struggled to her feet and picked up the robe.

'Okay, okay. Are you always this much of a bully?' But it felt good. Somebody else was making decisions. Someone was looking after her for a change. She swallowed the lump that rose in her throat. How long had it been?

When Kendrick left, she stepped into the shower and let the warm water wash over her. Her clothes were ruined, but she didn't care. At least she had been able to save a life today. There would be a family who wouldn't have to go through what she'd been through, and despite her exhaustion that felt good.

After her shower, she wrapped her hair in a towel turban style and slipped her robe back on. Kendrick would be back with food soon and she should really get dressed. But she had no energy to do that. All she wanted right now was to sleep. She prayed that for once it would be dreamless.

She pulled the over-large T-shirt she used as a nightie over her head and slipped into bed, pulling the sheets up to her chin. Surely not even Kendrick could mistake her actions for anything more than a desperate, overwhelming urge for rest? She closed her eyes, just for a moment. She would hear him return and then she'd persuade him that she was perfectly all right and just needed to be left alone.

Kendrick stood, tray in hand, looking down at Elizabeth. In sleep she looked younger, more vulnerable. Something shifted in his chest. He had started out wanting to sleep with her, but now? Now he wanted more. He found himself wanting to know more about her. And that hadn't happened for a long, long time.

She was beautiful but she didn't even seem to notice. He placed the tray on the floor and sat on the edge of the bed. Were those dried tears he saw on her cheeks? It surprised him. Until last night he would have said she was incapable of much emotion, she was so much the ice maiden. Yesterday at the hospital he'd seen a wave of sadness cross her face. But she had dealt with the bus crash calmly and efficiently. This was a woman he'd want around if ever he got into trouble in one of his stunts. Come to think of it, this was a woman he wanted around, period.

The thought took him by surprise. He was treading on dangerous ground, letting Elizabeth get under his skin.

He was about to creep away when she whispered, 'No!' For one crazy moment he thought she knew he was there and was begging him not to go, but she cried out the word again and fresh tears leaked from her eyes.

Then she was crying in earnest. Deep, racking sobs that shook her body. Instinctively he pulled her into his arms.

'Shh,' he whispered. 'Wake up, Lizzie. You're having a bad dream.'

Her eyes snapped open and what he saw there made him suck in a breath. He had never seen such naked pain before and it did something to his insides.

'Charlie,' she said urgently. 'I want Charlie.'

'Who is Charlie?' he asked.

The confusion in her eyes cleared and he saw that she had woken up from whatever dark place she'd been. Who was this Charlie?

'Kendrick?' She struggled to sit up, brushing the tears away from her cheeks with a trembling hand. 'What…what time is it?'

'It's seven,' he said. 'I brought you some food. I think you should eat something.'

She smiled wanly. 'A true knight in shining armour. Maybe I could just have a coffee.'

He stood back to let her get out of bed. She was wearing a too-big T-shirt that slipped off her shoulder, revealing an exquisite glimpse of the swell of her breasts. The T-shirt skimmed the tops of her thighs. He swallowed a groan. God, he wanted her. Had she not just a few moments ago been held in the grip of a nightmare he wouldn't have been able to stop himself from kissing her. But then she reached out for him and he was lost.

'Who is Charlie?' Kendrick asked much later. At his words she felt herself stiffen.

'Why do you ask?' She was sure she hadn't mentioned Charlie to him.

'You were dreaming when I brought you the food. You were crying and you said his name. Was he your ex-husband?'

Her blood chilled. She didn't want her past to have anything to do with this…whatever it was. If she told him about Charlie, it would change things. She wanted this to stay simple.

'No. Someone else.' *Forgive me, Charlie. I never thought I'd deny you.*

She turned around in his arms until she was facing him. 'I don't want to talk about Charlie,' she said. 'For whatever time we are together I want to pretend there is no past and not try to pretend there is a future. I want to live for the here and now. Can you accept that?'

His smile widened. 'Hey, that's usually my line.'

She leaned towards him, caught his bottom lip between her teeth and bit it gently. As his arms tightened about her she felt a flicker of triumph. It was her turn to make him crazy.

When Elizabeth woke again, the sun was shining through the curtains of her trailer and she was alone. Some time during the early hours of the morning she'd been aware of Kendrick kissing her and saying softly that he was going back to his trailer before the others arrived back.

She lifted her arms behind her head and stretched languorously. Then she glanced at the clock. Nine o'clock! She hadn't slept that late for years!

Leaping out of bed, she hurried to the shower.

Although there wouldn't be any filming today, it was possible one or more of the cast might have returned early and come looking for her. Finding their doctor in bed was not the image she wanted to engender.

As she lathered herself she thought back to the last couple of nights. The truth was it was difficult to think of anything but Kendrick. She sighed. Had she made a mistake, sleeping with him? It hadn't been planned but the need for comfort, the need to be held, the need to forget about her pain had been too strong. But that didn't explain the other times they had made love. She blushed at the memory. That had been pure lust.

By the time she emerged from her trailer she was feeling distinctly panicky. How would Kendrick behave towards her? Would he act as if nothing had happened? Would he ignore her—heaven forbid—or would he try to pick up where they'd left off? And what did she want? Damn. She felt like a girl with her first crush.

Kendrick looked up from his coffee as she entered the mess tent. He was chatting to Josh.

Her heart beating wildly, Elizabeth knew she

had no option but to join them. She just wished she didn't feel like a schoolgirl on her first date.

'Morning, Lizzie,' Kendrick greeted her, his eyes dancing. 'Did you sleep well?'

'Very well,' Elizabeth responded primly, hoping her face wasn't as red as it felt. 'Do you mind if I join you?' Now she knew she sounded as if she were at some tea party. The gleam in Kendrick's eye told her he was enjoying her discomfort.

'Of course.' Kendrick made space for her to sit next to him. 'We're just discussing one of our gags.'

'Gag?' Elizabeth was confused.

'It's what we stuntmen call the stuff we do.'

Suspecting she wouldn't like the answer, Elizabeth thought it best if she didn't ask why.

'So what is it?' she asked, taking a fork full of her scrambled egg.

'It involves a car crash and a hot burn,' Kendrick said, with a glance at Josh.

'A hot burn?' She was liking this conversation less and less.

'It's where I have to look as if I'm on fire,' Kendrick said. 'But don't worry,' he added hastily. 'We know what we're doing. We've done it before. We make sure there are folk around with fire extinguishers and I'll have stuff on that keeps the flames from burning.'

'As long as they get to you in two minutes,' Josh said darkly.

'They will,' Kendrick said.

It did nothing to allay Elizabeth's fears. It sounded as if there was a great deal that could go wrong. It was one thing watching Kendrick doing his stunts when she wasn't…what? Involved? Sleeping with him? Crazy about him? The thought stopped her breath. She wasn't crazy about him. She liked him. He was good for her at a time in her life when she wanted to pretend that she was someone else. That was all.

But the way he was looking at her and the way her heart responded—kicking against her ribs—made her wonder if that was true.

Confused, she realised she'd lost her appetite and pushed her plate away, reaching for her coffee instead.

'Are the others back yet?' she asked. She didn't want to think those thoughts.

'Some of them. The rest won't return until after lunch. In the meantime, Josh and I are going to go over the gags we'll be doing tomorrow.' He leaned back in his chair, looking like a man who was satisfied with life and no wonder.

'I'll make sure I'm around.' Elizabeth picked up her tray. 'What time?'

'Straight after we're finished here. We work it out on paper first then we build the stunt up bit by bit. You can stay and listen to how we do it, if you like.'

But Elizabeth was already on her feet. She wanted to get away from Kendrick and his searching looks so she could compose herself.

'I won't if you don't mind. I'm going to go to the medical trailer and see if anyone's looking for me. I also need to check my supplies.' She knew she was over-explaining but she didn't want him to know how much being near him was flustering her. She was beginning to think that not feeling was better than this acute anxiety coiling in the pit of her stomach.

Across on the other side of the set she was surprised to find Jack leaning against the door of the trailer. He was alone, which in itself was unusual. Every other time Elizabeth had seen him he had been followed by an entourage of assistants, make-up artists, stylists and who knew what else. They all shared one thing in common. Simpering adulation of the great man. Personally Elizabeth didn't get it. He might be rich, successful and good-looking—although not in the masculine way Kendrick was—and a film star, but he was arrogant and disinterested in anyone else to the point of rudeness sometimes. She wondered what had brought him to seek her out.

'Jack, what can I do for you?' Elizabeth asked, unlocking the door of her trailer.

For the first time he looked unsure of himself. He kicked a pebble away with the toe of one of his expensive shoes.

'Why don't you come in out of the heat?' she continued as Jack still didn't say anything.

'We missed you the other night,' Jack said eventually, flashing her the famous grin she had seen on the large screen many times before.

'I'm sorry. It sounded like a great night,' Elizabeth replied.

'I heard there was some sort of accident on the road up here last night and that you and Kendrick helped out. Is that right?'

Elizabeth nodded to a chair. 'Please, make yourself comfortable.' She was pretty sure he hadn't come to talk about the accident. 'Yes. It was a shock. Thankfully everyone we rescued is going to be all right. It was lucky Kendrick was there to help.'

'Ah, Kendrick. Our very own real-life hero.' Elizabeth didn't like the way he said it. He couldn't envy Kendrick, could he? She hid a smile. It was quite possible Jack didn't like the competition. He had made his money pretending to be a hero, whereas Kendrick really was one.

'Is it Kendrick you came to talk to me about?' she asked coolly. 'Or was there something else on your mind?'

Suddenly Jack paled. Elizabeth only just had enough time to grab a sick bowl before he doubled up and vomited violently.

She held his shoulders as he heaved. This was why he was alone. He'd hardly want anyone to see him like this.

Eventually, after Jack had stopped being sick and had wiped himself down with the cool cloth Elizabeth passed him, he sank back into the chair looking distraught.

'How long have you been feeling like this? Any other symptoms?' Elizabeth asked.

Jack nodded. 'I've been feeling this way for the last couple of hours. I must have been sick at least four times. Am I having a heart attack or something? I sure feel like hell.'

'I doubt you're having a heart attack. Far more likely it's something you ate. Perhaps in the last few days?' If so, it was unlikely Jack would be the only victim. 'Can you remember what you ate?'

'Lobster, oysters, salad, the beef, other things. A bit of salad.'

She had nibbled the lobster Kendrick had brought from the party. Come to think of it, her stomach was feeling decidedly queasy. Great. A set full of ill people and if she was right, only a sick doctor to look after them.

'I'm going to help you back to your trailer and make sure you're comfortable. If you don't stop being sick in a couple of hours I'll give you an anti-emetic to help, although if it is food poisoning it's best to let your system get rid of any toxins. I want you to take sips of water. If you can't keep that down, I'll give you some electrolyte fluid. Do you know if anyone else is having symptoms?'

She helped Jack to his feet. All his earlier bravado had disappeared. Now he was just another sick patient feeling understandably sorry for himself.

'I don't know. I haven't seen anyone else since I arrived back this morning. I sent my assistant away. I didn't want her around to see me being sick.'

As soon as she'd settled Jack she would go and check up on everyone else. It was possible others had been afflicted and were too ill to leave their trailers.

And she was right. There were at least four others in the same boat as Jack and no doubt others had yet to become ill. She phoned public health to let them know that there was an outbreak of food poisoning but as it had been most certainly from the food at a private party there was nothing they needed to do except be aware if any other family doctors phoned in to let them know about patients. Everyone who was ill had eaten the lobster and Elizabeth knew it was likely she would get ill herself. In the meantime, she needed to make sure that Philip was aware of what was going on.

As she crossed the camp to find the director, she passed Kendrick and Josh, who were practising some complicated-looking somersault on a trampoline, presumably to perfect it before shooting a stunt.

She walked over to them and waited until they had finished.Kendrick noticed her and came across straight away. 'We don't need you on standby just yet,' he said. 'I'll let you know when we start practising it in earnest.'

'Make sure you do. But that's not why I'm here. Did either of you have lobster at the party?'

Kendrick shook his head. 'Can't stand them. Taste of the sea and salt, that's all.'

'What about you, Josh?'

'Don't care much for them either. Give me a good steak any day.'

'Why are you wanting to know?' Kendrick asked. 'Don't tell me they were off?' He broke into a wide grin. 'I can't imagine Jack being best pleased about that. He likes to think he throws the best parties, not ones that make his guests sick.'

'It was probably just a bad one. But if you two are okay, I need to get on.' A spasm of pain sliced through her abdomen and she pressed her stomach with a hand. Perhaps she should give herself an anti-emetic? That might keep the symptoms at bay long enough for her to make sure everyone else was okay.

'Are you all right? Here, come and sit down.' Kendrick placed an arm around her shoulders and made to lead her away. Elizabeth shook her head and tried to push him away.

'You had the lobster too.' He was no longer smiling.

'I'll be okay.'

But before she could protest Kendrick swept her up in his arms and was striding across to her trailer.

'Will you put me down?' Elizabeth snarled, mortified. 'I have to see to my patients.' She could barely speak. Nausea was rising and her stomach was churning. Please, God, don't let me be sick. Not now, all over Kendrick and in front of everyone.

Kendrick kicked open the door of her trailer and placed her on her sofa.

'Okay. You stay here. Tell me what you want me to do.'

'Go and see who is ill and make sure that someone is looking after them.' As the nausea rose in her throat she pushed him towards the door. 'Go!'

Later that evening, when Elizabeth was beginning to feel a little more human and contemplating a shower, there was a knock on her door.

Without a shower, she wasn't in a fit state to see anyone. Her hair was matted, her make-up smudged and she had discarded her clothes on the floor and curled up in bed wearing only her bra and panties.

Before she had a chance to tell whoever it was to go away, the door opened and Kendrick strode in uninvited. She should've guessed. Even if she'd barred her doors and windows the man would probably still have found a way in. She wouldn't even put it past him to remove a door from its hinges if it got in his way.

'Go away, Kendrick,' she groaned, hiding her head under the blanket. 'I'm not human enough to have visitors. So unless you're here to tell me that someone needs my urgent medical attention, just go away—please.'

'I brought you some fruit juice,' he said. 'And I thought I should tell you there are about ten of you who are suffering from eating lobsters. I've coerced those of the cast who are okay into keeping an eye on the rest. Holding sick bowls isn't really my—er—thing. At least you don't have to worry about the others.'

There was silence for a moment and she wondered whether he had left. She peered over the top of the sheet and her heart stopped. He had picked up the photograph of Charlie she had left on the bedside table and was scrutinising it.

'Who is this?' he asked softly. Elizabeth had to resist the impulse to snatch the photo from his hand. Usually she left it in her drawer for exactly this reason. She didn't want unexpected visitors to her trailer asking questions she wasn't ready to answer. But she had taken it into bed with her when she'd been feeling so dreadful and at some point during the day had placed it back on the table next to her.

'It's my daughter. Charlie.'

'So this is Charlie. What happened to her, Lizzie?'

She held out her hand for the photograph and when Kendrick passed it back she traced Charlie's sweet face with the tip of her finger. She could hardly force the words past her closed throat.

'She died,' she said simply.

'Lizzie, I'm so sorry.' Kendrick sat down on the bed and pulled her towards him so that she was nestled against his chest. 'You don't have to tell me if you don't want to.'

But she did.

'She was born with Gauther's disease. It's a life-limiting illness. I knew almost from the start that she wasn't going to be with me very long.'

Kendrick said nothing but she felt his arms tighten around her.

'I gave up work to look after her. She needed full-time care and I wanted to do it myself. I wanted to spend every second of her life with her.' Her voice faltered and she sniffed loudly. 'She died three months ago. She was only eighteen months old. Kendrick, no mother should outlive her child. That's why I'll never have any more. I couldn't bear to go through that again.'

'What about her father? You said you were married?'

Elizabeth sighed. 'Simon? He couldn't take it that he had a child with disabilities. It was as if it was a slur on his manhood. Can you believe he wanted me to give her up for adoption? He said that way we could try for another. As if Charlie was a toy that could be thrown away just because she didn't live up to his expectations.' Anger pooled in her chest at the memory. 'I thought that Simon would come to accept Charlie, given some time, but he didn't. When I wouldn't hand Charlie over to foster-carers, he left.'

'He left you and Charlie alone?' Kendrick's voice was threaded with steel.

'We coped. You know, the next time I saw Simon was at Charlie's funeral.'

She shook her head. 'I could have forgiven him for leaving if only he'd kept in touch with Charlie. But once he walked out of the door, it was as if she—we—no longer existed for him.'

She managed a shaky breath. 'So you can see I'm serious about never marrying again. I'd rather be on my own than go through that again. It's simpler.'

'Not all men are like your ex-husband,' Kendrick said, but there was something in his voice that made Elizabeth's blood chill. He sounded distant, unlike the man she had shared her bed with.

He stood. 'I'd better get going.'

He looked down at her. There was a wariness in his expression that hadn't been there before. 'I'll come and check on you later.'

As Elizabeth had expected, the food poisoning took around twenty-four hours before everyone was over the worst, herself included. Kendrick kept popping in through the day to see how she was and to bring her news of the other afflicted members of cast and crew, but something had definitely shifted between them. He was friendly but the teasing spark in his eyes was gone.

And it made her feel like she'd been kicked in the ribs.

So much for telling herself that she didn't feel anything apart from lust for Kendrick. What an idiot she'd been. All she could hope for now was to salvage some pride. She wouldn't let him see that he'd hurt her, not even if it took all her acting skills. At least he wouldn't have that satisfaction.

He told her that Philip, who, like Kendrick, had been unaffected, was carrying on filming with those who were still on their feet.

'Not one to waste any time. Not that I can blame

him. Every day we're not filming costs money.'
He peered at her. 'You look as if you're on the
mend.'

Elizabeth felt as if a steamroller had run over
her and then reversed and done the same thing
again. Kendrick, on the other hand, looked dis-
gustingly healthy. Gorgeously, sexily, healthy.

She struggled to her feet. 'I'm going to see how
everyone is,' she said. 'No, really, Kendrick, I'm
fine,' she added as he looked about to protest.
'You've been really sweet, but I need to get on
and do my job.'

Kendrick looked doubtful for a moment then he
must have seen the determination in her face as
he stood aside. Good, she had managed just the
right tone.

'Okay, Lizzie. Have it your own way. I really
need to get on and do some practice with Josh.
Philip wants to film a stunt tonight, I'm afraid.
Whether you're fit to be there or not.'

'I'll be there,' Elizabeth muttered. 'Just let
anyone try and stop me.'

Later that afternoon, after she'd made sure all the
afflicted patients were recovering, Elizabeth wan-

dered over to where they were setting up for the stunt. She still felt weak but she knew by the time tomorrow came she'd be almost back to normal. Jack had insisted on being flown back to LA as soon as he had stopped vomiting and was expected back in a day or two.

'Without my lead man, I need to get as many of these stunts in the bag as we can,' Philip was saying. 'At least then I won't lose too much time.' He glared at Elizabeth as if it was all her fault. Kendrick winked at her behind Philip's back.

'What about if we do the car-chase scene out in the desert?' Kendrick suggested. 'Josh and I have that one pretty much worked out.' He sketched a wave behind him. 'I know what I have to do with the burning building. That can wait until Jack is back.'

Philip looked somewhat appeased.

'How about you, Doc?' he asked Elizabeth. 'Are you up to being around?'

Kendrick frowned. 'I'd forgotten the doctor needed to be there. I'm not sure it's a good idea for her to be standing around in the sun when she's been ill.'

'I'll be fine.' Although Kendrick was intervening for the best of reasons, she wasn't about to let him tell her how to do her job. How would he feel if she tried to tell him how to do his? She suppressed a smile at the thought of her directing his stunts. If she had her way he'd jump from no more than two feet off the ground and somehow she doubted that was going to happen. However, it felt good that someone cared enough to think about her welfare. It had been so long since anyone had. The thought jolted her. She was used to coping on her own. Did she really want someone to involve themselves in her life?

'Good,' Philip said before Kendrick could protest further. 'Let's get the crew that are okay on their feet and out of here. I want to film the scene while there's good light.'

'I'll go and get my medical bag,' Elizabeth said, turning towards her trailer.

Kendrick fell into step alongside her.

'Are you sure you're up to it?' he asked. 'Because I could refuse to do it today and he'll have no option but to postpone it.'

Elizabeth stopped in her tracks and faced him. 'Kendrick, I appreciate your help and your...' she sought for the right word '...concern. But I'm as professional as you. If I'm needed, I'll be there. Don't worry, I'll take a hat and plenty of water, as well as extra for everyone.'

Kendrick looked far from being reassured. 'It'll be a long day.'

'And I'll be fine. Go and do whatever you need to while I get organised.' She looked at him for a long moment. 'This stunt is going to be safe, isn't it?' It was different from watching him before. Before what? She'd slept with him? Started to care about him? She shook her head, dismissing the thought. She didn't care about him in *that* way. *Don't you?* a little voice whispered. *You don't tend to sleep with men you don't care about. Who are you trying to kid?* She was determined she was going to ignore the voice. She could not afford to care about anyone. Not ever.

Kendrick was grinning at her. 'I'll make a deal with you. You let me look after my side and I'll let you look after yours.' He placed a hand on her shoulder. 'Don't worry, Lizzie, we make the stunts as safe as possible. It's my job to look out for Josh and make sure he stays in one piece. He used to drive rally cars for a living. He's the best there is, you have my word for it. We only need you there as insurance.'

It took another hour before the trucks were loaded and ready to go. Philip had explained that it would be a chase across the desert, culminating in a crash of the car Josh was driving, as Jack's double, into a lorry that would be parked on the side of the road. None of that reassured Elizabeth. What if something went badly wrong? They had the helicopter standing by with a pilot to airlift Josh to hospital should the need arise. She hoped it wouldn't be. She'd inspected the helicopter thoroughly when she'd first arrived. It had a defibrillator as well as monitoring equipment and oxygen. She had to admit it was as well equipped as anything she'd encountered when she'd worked as a member of the BASICs team. But that had been different. There she had been part of a team. Here she was on her own. Here she was expected to look after people who, for all her determination to keep her distance from them, she was beginning to think of as her friends. And that was without whatever it was she felt for Kendrick.

Nevertheless, she knew she could handle most eventualities. And hadn't Kendrick promised her that he was safety conscious? Apart from the odd cut and bruise, so far he had shown himself pretty adept at minimising any damage to himself.

One of the crew, a woman called Julie who was one of the sound recordists, came to stand next to her. Elizabeth offered her a drink of water and Julie took it gratefully.

'Some heat, huh? The weathermen keep promising it's going to get cooler.'

Elizabeth wiped her brow. 'Can't come soon enough for me.'

They watched together as Kendrick strapped Josh in the driver's seat of the car.

'Have you worked with Kendrick and Josh before?' Elizabeth asked.

'Kendrick, about five times. He's one of the best at what he does so the directors like to use him. Josh, I think I might have worked with once before. The stuntmen tend to keep themselves to themselves on a set as a rule. Kendrick is a bit unusual in that he mixes more.' She sighed. 'He's so gorgeous. I keep hoping he'll ask me out, but so far no luck. Perhaps he's got an eye on Tara. He usually goes for the female lead.'

A shock ran through Elizabeth's body that felt

uncomfortably like jealousy. Why was she surprised? Kendrick had made no secret of the fact he liked female company.

'He and Tara had a fling a couple of years ago. It lasted the whole of the time we were filming, but then it seemed to peter out. I guess Kendrick isn't in it for the long term. Do you know stuntmen are just as likely to get divorced as stars?' Julie took a final swig of her water. 'Oh, well, I suppose I'd better get back to work.'

The nausea had returned. Was Julie trying to send her a not-so-subtle warning? Had people noticed that there was something between Kendrick and herself?

It was one thing thinking she knew about Kendrick, quite another hearing that she was no more than another notch in his bedpost. Anxiety and anger coiled in her stomach. She'd been an idiot to let him get under her guard. On the other hand, it wasn't as if he'd forced her. In fact, hadn't it been his lack of commitment that had attracted her in the first place? Why, then, did she feel so bereft?

CHAPTER SEVEN

BY THE next day, the camp was crowded with cast and crew once more. Jack still hadn't returned but everyone was in good spirits after their short break and there was a buzz of excitement.

'Okay, folks, gather round.' Philip's megaphone was back in action and even the usually surly director appeared in good form. Once everyone was assembled he lowered his megaphone.

'I think we have only a couple of weeks left before it's a wrap.'

A cheer went up at his words, but Elizabeth felt a sinking sensation in her chest. Soon Kendrick would be out of her life for good. She still hadn't decided what to do when filming finished, although she had sent a letter to her former employers to ask whether there was a vacancy for her.

Once filming was under way, Elizabeth strolled across to her medical trailer.

This morning there were more than the usual one or two patients waiting. She dealt with a sprained ankle, a mild chest infection and a bad rash. When the last patient had left, she heard a tap on the door. It was Tara. They hadn't spoken much but when they had, Elizabeth had found the actress self-deprecating and witty.

'Hi, Elizabeth, I had a few moments free so I thought I'd come and find you,' Tara said.

'Is there anything wrong?' Elizabeth asked.

'Not really,' Tara said evasively. 'I just wondered if you had a pregnancy test.'

'Of course,' Elizabeth said. 'How sure are you?'

'Pretty sure. I've been pregnant twice before so I know the symptoms. I'm two weeks late, and I'm never late.'

Elizabeth reached into a drawer and handed Tara a couple of tests.

'I didn't know you had children.'

'I have a son. He stays with his dad when I'm filming. I miscarried my last pregnancy.'

Tara's eyes filled and Elizabeth reached for her hand. 'I'm so sorry.'

'It happens, or so they tell me. I just hope nothing happens to this one. If the test is positive.'

'There is no reason at all if you've had one healthy baby why you shouldn't have another. And I'll be here to keep an eye on you. Why don't you nip into my bathroom and do the test and then I can check your blood pressure? Unless, of course, you'd rather be on your own when you do it. I suspect your husband might want to be the first to hear.'

'I don't want to tell him. I don't want him to know. If I am pregnant I want to get beyond the first twelve weeks before I get his hopes up.'

'That's a big thing to ask of yourself, not to have anyone to share your anxiety with. Look, go do the test and if it's positive we can chat some more.'

While Tara was in the bathroom, Elizabeth closed her eyes and remembered. The dizzy excitement when she'd thought she was pregnant. Doing the test and seeing the blue line. Stopping herself from phoning Simon at work, but instead getting off work early, wanting the moment to be perfect when she told him. They had been trying for a couple of years and were just about to embark on a course of IVF when she'd fallen pregnant naturally. Since then she'd thought of Charlie as her miracle baby.

On the way home from work, she'd been unable to stop herself going into a toyshop and buying a snowy-white, baby-soft Jemima Puddleduck with her jaunty blue hat and scarf. The books of Beatrix Potter had been her favourite when she'd been a child.

At home, she had done everything she'd always read about. Cooked a meal. Set the table with candles. Placed Mrs Puddleduck on the bedside table, not wanting to give the game away too soon.

She had hardly contained herself until Simon had come home. One look at her face had been enough. He had danced her around the room and later, after they had eaten, they had sat in front of the fire wrapped in each other's arms, dreaming about the future. Discussing how this time next year there would be three of them. And maybe in another couple of years another child. Her life had seemed so perfect back then.

Tara emerged from the bathroom, a nervous smile on her face.

'Positive. It says positive. But I think I should do another one, just to be sure.'

The second one was also positive, as Elizabeth knew it would be. She spoke to Tara, established she had been taking folic acid and that during her first successful pregnancy she hadn't any problems.

'From your dates I think you must be about six weeks,' Elizabeth said. 'There's no point in having a scan until you're a bit further on, but I can arrange that for you if you like. Or you can see your own ob/gyn when you're next in town. Come to think of it, that might be best. He or she knows your obstetric history.'

'But you can look after me while I'm here?' Tara said. 'That would be okay, won't it? My ob/gyn is a friend of my husband.'

'He won't be able to tell your husband anything without your express permission,' Elizabeth said.

'I know, but I'd rather not take the chance that he wouldn't let it slip.'

Elizabeth took one of Tara's hands in hers. 'I think you should reconsider telling your husband, you know. That's what they're there for.'

As she said the words she knew that in her case, at least, it had been a lie. Simon had been totally unable to support her when she'd needed him most. She would never make the mistake on counting on anyone else ever again. Not that she planned ever to need anyone's support. Her life, with just her in it, was her business and how she lived it was up to her and her alone.

'I'll think about it,' Tara said. 'I promise.'

She laughed as the sound of Philip on his megaphone blasted though the walls of the trailer. 'I think we're being summoned.'

Back on set, Kendrick and the rest of his team were in a huddle, setting up the next stunt.

'He's cute, don't you think?' Tara said, watching Elizabeth from the corner of her heavily made-up eyes. 'He and I were together a few years ago, before I met my husband. It didn't last long but while it did, it was fun.'

Elizabeth felt something uncomfortably like jealousy coil in her chest.

'I need to get to Make-up,' Tara excused herself. 'I'll see you later.'

As Tara walked away, Elizabeth watched Kendrick do the stunt they had been setting up. Now she knew what the practising with the trampoline had been about. Kendrick used it to gain enough height to do a somersault just as Josh and some of the other members of the crew let off a mock explosion. From where she was standing it all looked very real. As if Kendrick really had been blown up and had been sent flying by the force of the explosion.

After the third take, Kendrick caught her looking at him and for one long moment their eyes locked.

She thought she saw something in his eyes but then the shutters came down and he turned away. A chill ran up her spine. Had Tara been right to warn her? Now Kendrick had slept with her, was he regretting it? Preparing to move on to his next conquest? A wave of anger washed over her. That was up to him. Neither of them had made any promises, but she was damned if she was going to be fobbed off like some unwelcome guest at a party. She made up her mind. She would speak to him, make it clear he had nothing to fear on that score. She was grown up and was perfectly able to deal with what had happened like an adult, and she would make damn sure he gave her the same courtesy.

Kendrick was sitting outside his trailer, carving a piece of wood and whistling under his breath.

He jumped to his feet when he saw her coming towards him.

'Lizzie. How're you doing?'

'I'm fine.' She sucked in a breath. 'Kendrick, can we talk?'

'Sure,' he said, drawing up a chair for her to sit. The wary look was back in his eyes.

Elizabeth looked around. The set was teaming with people visiting one another, walking around or playing a board game under the outside lights of their trailers. Others were sharing a beer at the makeshift bar.

'Not here,' she said. 'Let's take a walk.'

Kendrick got to his feet without saying anything and they walked into the desert in silence until they had left the camp behind.

Taking a deep breath, Elizabeth turned to face him. 'You've been avoiding me. Do you want to tell me why?'

Kendrick looked at her with cool blue eyes. There was no trace of his usual grin.

'Lizzie…' he started to say, then stopped. 'No, you're right. I have been avoiding you,' he said at last. 'I refuse to play games with you.'

Elizabeth propped her hands on her hips.

'Have you decided that sleeping with me was a mistake? Because I have to tell you, Kendrick, I'm a big girl.'

For a moment the smile was back. 'No, sleeping with you wasn't a mistake,' he said. 'It's just… Look, Lizzie, I wanted to make love to you, I thought we could, you know, have something going for a while. We're both adults. We knew what we were doing.'

'So?'

'But that was before I knew about Charlie.'

'And just what does Charlie have to do with it?'

'You're vulnerable. Lizzie, your child died only a few months ago. I would never have slept with you had I known.'

Anger flooded Elizabeth's body. 'When do you get to decide what is right for me and what isn't? Where do you get off deciding whether I'm too vulnerable to sleep with you? Who gives you the right to decide? Kendrick, if you want to end it, at least have the decency to be truthful.'

'I wanted to make love to you, Lizzie. Not feel responsible.'

For a moment she wanted to take a swing at him. 'Feel responsible for me?' She almost spat the words. 'What the hell makes you think I want anyone to feel responsible for me? I told you about Charlie because you asked. Would you have preferred me to keep her a secret? Would that have made you feel better?'

'Lizzie…' He reached for her but she stepped back. She was so angry she could feel the blood pumping in her veins.

'You caught me at a vulnerable moment, I'll give you that. But I slept with you because I wanted to. I slept with you because it helped me blot out the pain, even if it was only for a short while. Do you have any idea how much I ache inside?'

'Lizzie…' Even in the moonlight she could see that he had paled. He stepped towards her again, but she didn't want him near her.

'You think that wanting comfort means I want you in my life permanently? You couldn't be more wrong. I will never marry again. I will never love again. I will never have another child. So don't you dare tell me what I want.' She was breathing hard. The tightness in her chest was getting stronger.

'I can look after myself. I want to look after myself. I will never rely on another man again.

Least of all you.' She took a deep, steadying breath. 'We had sex, Kendrick. That was all. Don't make it into something it wasn't.'

She turned on her heel, knowing that if she didn't get back to the safety of her trailer, she would break down in front of him, and that was the last thing she wanted. It would just confirm to Kendrick everything he thought. That she was vulnerable. The word made her temper rise all over again and she whirled back to face him.

'And stop calling me Lizzie.'

Kendrick watched her furious figure stomp away. That hadn't gone well. Despite being taken aback by her anger, he felt a smile tug at his lips. Why had he ever thought she was an ice maiden? She was a tiger when she got going.

He stared out into the desert. What he'd told Elizabeth hadn't been exactly the truth, but he could hardly have told her the real reason he was keeping his distance from her. When she'd told him about her daughter Charlie, he'd wanted nothing more than to pull her into his arms and protect her from ever being hurt again. He prided himself in not being afraid of anything—but that kind of emotion scared him witless. He didn't want anyone to rely on him. He didn't want anyone to expect anything of him. He had no illusions. He wasn't the kind of man a woman should marry. He didn't want children, he'd be a lousy father and he wasn't going to subject a child to that. Look at how things had turned out between him and his father. All his father had ever wanted was a carbon copy of himself. Someone to follow in his footsteps. Someone to make him proud. And Kendrick had failed on all counts. He was done with failing people. And the best way to do that was by not making promises he couldn't keep.

He rubbed his chin.

But Elizabeth was different. She no more wanted a relationship, a future, than he did. Then he felt a moment's chagrin. She had slept with him for comfort? That didn't sit well either. He wanted her to have slept with him for the same reasons he had wanted her. Because of over-whelming lust.

He kicked at a stone with the tip of his boot. He believed every word that she'd said. She didn't want a long-term relationship. After all, she'd said she could look after herself. That was abundantly clear. Why, then, did he feel this strange sense of disappointment?

CHAPTER EIGHT

HEARING raised voices, Elizabeth looked across to the other side of the camp. A woman with long black hair was standing in front of Kendrick with her hands on her hips, shouting something Elizabeth couldn't quite make out while gesticulating to a Jeep parked behind her. Even from this distance Elizabeth could tell that whatever she was saying wasn't making Kendrick very happy. Intrigued, Elizabeth wandered over to them.

'He's your flesh and blood too,' the dark-haired woman was shouting. 'Don't you think it's time you helped out?'

'I'm working.' Kendrick folded his arms.

The woman reached into the back of the car, reappearing a few moments later with a child in her arms. Judging by its size, it couldn't have been more than eighteen months old.

'It's just for today. You can take him to the ranch

tomorrow and I'll collect him from there. C'mon, Kendrick, you owe me.'

Elizabeth's mouth was dry. It looked as if the woman doing the shouting was an ex-lover of Kendrick's. Dropping off the child with his father. And from what she was saying it seemed Kendrick hadn't taken much responsibility. The realisation made her feel ill. If ever she needed proof that Kendrick was just like Simon, here it was.

The woman pushed the child towards Kendrick, who was forced to accept the toddler. Kendrick held it at arm's length, a look of puzzlement on his face. Clearly he had no idea what to do with the little person he had been handed.

Appalled, Elizabeth watched as the woman jumped into her Jeep and with a flurry of dust drove away. Turning on her heel, Elizabeth headed back to her trailer.

Inside she sat on her bed, trying to get her thumping heart under control. Kendrick had a child, one that he was clearly trying to avoid taking responsibility for. He was a snake. Not much better than Simon, and it was good she had discovered this now. What had she been thinking when she'd thought he was different? Her judgement when it came to men was clearly flawed.

She stood up and began to pace. Okay, so she had misjudged Kendrick. Where did that leave her? She had coped on her own before and she could do so again.

She picked up the photograph of Charlie and held it to her. Her heart ached as she remembered her little girl looking up at her with trusting eyes, relying on Mummy to take the pain away, to make everything better. But she hadn't been able to. She'd had no option but to watch Charlie suffer. And that despicable man outside couldn't even be bothered to look after his child for one day. More importantly, could she let another child of hers go through that again?

Hating the way she felt disappointed in Kendrick, realising now how much she'd wanted him to be different and wondering if she'd ever be able to look at another child without feeling torn in two, Elizabeth sat down on the bed and sobbed.

Once she had cried herself out, she washed her face and repaired her make-up. She still had a job to do. Filming was due to start and after that she would be in her trailer for any of the cast who needed medical advice. Whatever she decided to do, whatever agonies of indecision she was going through would have to be put aside until she was alone again.

Walking back onto the set, she saw that whoever the woman with the child was had got her way. Kendrick was sitting outside his trailer, looking on with bemusement as Josh walked up and down, trying to comfort the child, who was screaming as if its heart would break.

Whatever Josh was trying to do clearly wasn't working. The cries ripped through Elizabeth and she tried to close her ears. This wasn't her problem. Hadn't she come here so that she wouldn't have to face children? Steeling her heart, she went to pass by but Josh called out to her.

'Doc, could you help us here? I think Kip is in pain. Something serious has to be up with the kid.'

Elizabeth stopped in her tracks and sighed. She had no choice. It was possible that the child was in pain, although she doubted it. The cries sounded much more like those of a toddler who was over-tired or hungry, or both. Nevertheless, whatever her own feelings, she couldn't stand by and ignore a distressed infant.

'Let me have a look,' she said.

Kendrick was waving his car keys in front of the child's face, but if he thought that was going to do anything to calm it down he was badly mistaken. Instead, the cries rose in pitch and the little face screwed up with fury.

Elizabeth removed the screaming infant from Josh's arms. Almost immediately, as if the child knew he was in the hands of someone who knew what they were doing, the cries tailed off. Brown eyes fixed on hers.

'Name?' Elizabeth said brusquely. The familiar feel of a small warm body in her arms, the particular baby smell, the familiar look of trust and entreaty, was breaking her up inside.

'Kip,' Kendrick said. 'What's up with him? I didn't know something that small could make a sound so loud.' He pulled a hand through his hair. In the time that Elizabeth had been gone he seemed to have aged. He wasn't the cool, collected Kendrick of earlier. In his place was a man who looked at the end of his tether.

'I think Kip might be hungry, or sleepy, or—' she wrinkled her nose as the smell of ammonia drifted up her nostrils '—wet. Most likely all three. Do you have nappies? Food?'

Kendrick looked around as if expecting to find those things behind him. He turned impassioned eyes on Elizabeth. 'Where am I supposed to find those things?'

'What about the bag Kendall left for you?' Josh interrupted. He was looking more relaxed now that Elizabeth had appeared.

'Oh, yes. Of course.' Kendrick lifted a small leather bag from the ground next to him. 'I think it's all in here.'

Elizabeth balanced a hiccupping Kip on her hip and dug around in the bag. There were disposable nappies, bottles and a change of clothes. She hauled out one of the bottles and handed it to Josh. 'Could you get some boiled water and add it to the powder? Then bring it back. C'mon, Kendrick, let's go inside so you can change your son.' At his look of incredulity she snapped, 'You'll have to learn some time.' She was so angry with him she could barely talk.

'Son?' Kendrick said. Then he laughed. 'You think that bundle of fury belongs to me? You have to be kidding.'

'He's not yours?' Elizabeth tried to ignore the feeling of relief that swept through her.

'He's my nephew,' Kendrick said. 'His mother, my sister, just dumped him on me. Said she has an audition she just can't miss. I'm to take him to my parents' ranch. Apparently my harebrained sister didn't have time.'

'Then,' Elizabeth said firmly, 'he does belong to you. As his uncle it's your responsibility to look after him.' She walked into his trailer, leaving him to follow.

It was the first time she'd been inside his trailer and she looked around with interest. Almost the mirror image of hers, it was tidy. A guitar was set against a wall, the bed neatly made and the counter clear of dishes. It reminded her of army barracks. Clearly his time in the forces had left its mark on Kendrick.

She placed a tearstained Kip on the sofa and undid his nappy. She handed the sodden bundle to Kendrick, who couldn't have treated it with more dismay had she passed him a hand grenade.

She used the wipes she had found in the bag Kendall had left and soon had Kip a clean nappy. As she worked, the child's large brown eyes clung to hers and she found herself talking to him in a low, soothing voice.

'It's okay, baby. We'll soon have you feeling all comfy again. Then we'll give you your bottle and you can have a sleep. Mummy will be back tomorrow and in the meantime Uncle Kendrick...' she slid a look at Uncle Kendrick, who was watching her with a confused look on his face '...will look after you.'

'Can't you?' Kendrick said helplessly. 'I mean, I don't know how to look after a baby. Besides, I have to work. How can I work while looking after a baby? It's just not possible.'

'When did you last see your nephew, Kendrick?' Elizabeth asked. 'Doesn't he know you at all?'

'I saw him after he was born. He's changed since then. I would hardly know this is the same kid.'

'Then you'll have to learn how to look after him. At least until you take him to your parents'. I have to work too, so I can't look after him for you.'

Not just wouldn't—couldn't. Every moment she spent with this baby was tearing her in two.

Josh arrived back holding a full bottle of formula triumphantly. 'Sorted,' he said. 'What do we do now?'

Elizabeth chose to ignore that 'we'—at least for the time being. For now, she needed to ensure Kip was fed and put down for a nap. After that it was up to Kendrick.

She tested the milk on the inside of her wrist. Too hot. It needed a few minutes to cool down.

She pointed to Kendrick and then to the single armchair in the room. 'Sit there.'

Kendrick looked mutinous, but did as he was told.

Elizabeth placed Kip in his arms, and her heart cracked a little as the tiny boy was dwarfed in Kendrick's muscular arms. He was holding the child away from his body as if unsure what to do with him. Elizabeth suppressed a smile.

'He's not a sack of potatoes or live ammunition, you know. Hold him close to you.' She leaned over Kendrick and adjusted the child in his arms until he was lying snugly against Kendrick's chest. Kip smiled at his uncle, revealing two front teeth.

'Hey, did you see that?' Kendrick said, a note of wonder in his voice. 'The kid actually smiled at me. I think he likes me. Hey, kid, maybe later

I can take you for a ride. Would you like that? Go on a horse with your Uncle Kendrick?'

'He's too small to go on a horse, Kendrick,' Elizabeth said. 'Here's his bottle. Tip it up so he doesn't suck on air.'

Kendrick did as he was told and soon Kip was sucking hungrily. Elizabeth watched them for a moment. The sight of macho Kendrick holding the little boy was incongruous, yet melted her inside. This was how he would be with his own child. Eventually. Once he had some training. And if that child wasn't disabled. She couldn't imagine someone as sure of his own masculinity, so physical, coping with a child who wasn't. She could barely see him with a child who was fit and healthy.

Kendrick glowered at Josh, who was standing watching with a broad smile on his face. 'If you so much as breathe a whisper of this to the others, I'll have your guts.'

'Hey, you're a natural. What is there to be em-barrassed about?'

Kendrick tried to squint at his watch without disturbing the feeding child. 'We need to be on set in ten minutes.' He looked hopefully at Elizabeth. 'Do you think he'll be finished by then?'

'What? So you can leave him sleeping in the trailer? On his own?'

'Hell, I never thought of that. I don't suppose you…?'

'No, Kendrick. I have my own job to do. I can't look after a child.' Can't. Won't. Didn't want to. 'He's your responsibility. All yours.'

'I wonder if Imogen will look after him.'

'Imogen is in the next take,' Josh said. 'You're not.'

'In that case, I'll have to bring him on to the set with us. There must be something we can put him in.'

Elizabeth was exasperated. Did Kendrick really have no idea? But as long as the child came to no harm, it was none of her business. As she turned to leave them to it, she couldn't resist another quick peek. Now that he was fed and changed, Kip's eyes had softened and half closed as he surrendered to sleep.

Elizabeth swallowed the lump in her throat. Although she knew she could never risk having another child, it didn't mean she didn't long for another baby deep down inside. She blinked away the hot tears that burned behind her eyes. Hadn't she resolved to make the best of her life, to make the most of the cards she'd been dealt? There was no point in wishing for what she could never have.

Later that afternoon Elizabeth found herself in a Jeep with Kendrick and Kip. Not for the first time, she wondered why she'd let Kendrick persuade her to come with them to the ranch. The reason she had given herself—that she couldn't leave a defenceless child to the ministrations of his uncle—wasn't entirely true. She was curious to see where Kendrick had been brought up. But that wasn't totally true either. She was here because she wanted to be with Kendrick. Filming was due to finish soon and then Kendrick would walk out of her life for good. The thought was almost unbearable. How could she have let herself fall for this man? Hadn't she sworn to herself that she would never depend on anyone again, never lay herself open to being hurt? Yet here she was with a man who could only break her heart. And do it without noticing.

'Here we are,' Kendrick said as they turned

into a dust road. His face was set, his usual grin absent. He didn't look happy about being home.

Elizabeth couldn't see anything that looked like a ranch. All she could see were miles of fields with horses feeding contentedly.

'Hey, Kip. Do you see the horses?' Kendrick asked. But Kip was too busy looking the other way. At a clump of grass or a tree that must have caught his attention.

'Are they yours?' Elizabeth asked.

'My father's,' Kendrick said tightly. 'He owns around thirty. Some he uses for stud, the others on the ranch.'

'So he's a cowboy,' Elizabeth said, trying to make Kendrick smile. She was nervous enough, without dealing with the tension that was rolling from Kendrick in waves.

'Mmm. He doesn't do much of that. Luckily he leaves it to the guys who know what they're doing.'

After driving for another ten minutes along the bumpy track they pulled up outside a low-slung, sprawling ranch house. In front of the house and to their right was a paddock where a man who looked every inch a cowboy was standing in the centre as a horse galloped in a circle around him on a long rope. Every now and again the horse would lift its rear legs and kick the air as if frustrated.

Kendrick leaped out of the car and called over. 'Hey, Tim, how's it going?' He reached into the back seat and with some difficulty removed Kip from his baby seat. Holding him awkwardly in his arms, he went over and opened the car door for Elizabeth. It was on the tip of her tongue to tell him she was perfectly able to manage opening a car door herself but she bit back the words.

'Let's go and see what Tim's up to,' Kendrick said.

Elizabeth had no idea whether he was addressing her or the toddler but followed him across to the paddock fence. Kendrick perched Kip on the fence so he could see what was happening.

The horse reared when he saw them and Tim struggled to hold onto the rope.

'Looks like you need a hand there,' Kendrick said. A smile was playing in the corner of his mouth.

'He's a tough one,' Tim grunted. 'I've been trying to get a saddle on him this last week, but he's having none of it.'

'Could you hold Kip for a bit?' Kendrick asked. Before Elizabeth had time to protest, Kendrick was holding Kip towards her and she had no choice but to take the toddler from him. Kip reached out a chubby fist and grabbed the front of Elizabeth's blouse, twisting around so he could follow Kendrick with his eyes.

The feeling of the child in her arms made her throat tighten.

Kendrick vaulted over the fence and strode towards Tim. 'He doesn't trust you yet,' he said. 'Want me to give it a go?'

'You're the boss man,' Tim said. 'If anyone can get him to settle, it'll be you.'

The horse had come to a halt and was breathing heavily, its flanks tipped with frothy sweat. As Kendrick walked towards him the horse sidestepped and rolled his eyes.

'Hey, big fellow,' Kendrick said softly. 'No one's going to hurt you. No one's going to make you do anything you don't want to.'

The horse lowered its head and snorted, still eyeing Kendrick warily. Elizabeth held her breath. If the horse reared and caught Kendrick with one of its hooves, it could be nasty. Very nasty. She wanted to call him back, but she forced herself to swallow the words. Any sudden noise might make the horse react and do the very thing she dreaded. Kip was pointing and saying a stream of words in his own baby language. Elizabeth found herself squeezing him tighter. The warm body tucked against her felt painfully good.

Kendrick was still approaching the horse, talking quietly. As he spoke the horse calmed, its snorting and rolling eyes becoming still. Its ears pricked up and it looked at Kendrick. Tim had backed away before vaulting over the fence, and came to stand next to Elizabeth.

'Hey, Kip,' he said. 'How d'you do, ma'am?' He tipped a finger to his hat, making Elizabeth smile. It seemed as if she'd moved from one movie set to another.

Men were beginning to gather around. Without saying anything, except nodding in Elizabeth's direction, they positioned themselves along the fence to watch Kendrick.

'Bet you fifty dollars he doesn't get the saddle on Satan,' one of the watching ranch hands said to Tim.

Satan? The horse was called Satan. Elizabeth

was torn between covering her eyes or Kip's so that they wouldn't have to watch.

'Bet you a hundred he saddles him and rides him,' Tim said calmly.

'Ain't no one can ride that crazy animal. Not even Kendrick,' the man replied. 'But if you want to throw your money away, don't let me stop you.'

There was a flurry of activity while money changed hands. It seemed that all the watching men wanted to bet on whether Kendrick would be killed. If Elizabeth could have stopped this, she would have. On the other hand, she had seen enough of Kendrick in action to know that if anyone could do what the men were betting on, it would be him.

By this time Kendrick was stroking Satan's neck, still talking in a low voice. The horse nickered and tossed its head, but otherwise remained calm.

Kendrick held the rope near the horse's head and walked him around for a little while.

'Can you bring me a saddle?' he called over to Tim.

Tim cast a told-you-so look at the others and, picking up a saddle from the fence, carried it across to Kendrick. Satan skipped sideways again as he approached but Kendrick soothed him until he was standing still again. Kendrick waited until Tim was once more on the other side of the fence before he placed the saddle on the horse's back.

Elizabeth held her breath. Kip moved his hand and grabbed hold of her bottom lip and clung on for dear life. Elizabeth was too mesmerised at what was happening a few yards away to try and move his hand.

Feeling the weight of the saddle, Satan rose on his hind legs, scrabbling at the air with his front hooves and only narrowly missing Kendrick's head.

Undeterred, Kendrick waited until he calmed a little. There was another flurry of movement beside her as more money changed hands.

Then, with one easy movement, Kendrick leaped onto Satan's back. This time the horse reacted. Bucking and rearing as he broke into a canter. But Kendrick held on. Round and round they went until the horse stopped bucking and settled into a smoother gait. Then Kendrick turned Satan towards the fence and with an almost undetectable movement of his feet sent the horse soaring up and over the fence and into the plains stretching into the distance. As horse and rider disappeared there was a collective sigh from everyone watching.

'Okay, everyone, pay up and get back to work,' Tim said, holding out his hand.

'Will they be okay?' Elizabeth asked. 'I mean, what if Kendrick comes off? What if he hurts himself?' She tried to act as if her concern was nothing more than the natural concern of one human for another but judging by the speculative look in Tim's eyes he wasn't convinced.

'Don't worry about Kendrick. He'll be fine. If Satan tosses him, he knows how to fall. He'll be okay. Satan will come back and I'll send one of the lads to look for Kendrick. But as I said, I don't think that'll happen.' While he was talking he was counting the money in his hand with a satisfied smile. 'Those boys don't know Kendrick the way I do, otherwise they would never have bet against him.' He seemed to remember his manners. 'Come inside out of the heat, ma'am. I'll get you and Kip here a drink.'

'Have you known Kendrick long?' Elizabeth asked as they walked towards the house.

Tim's face lit up in a smile. 'Ever since he was

about Kip's age. He learned to ride almost as soon as he could walk. Always had a way with horses too. Seems he can talk to them in a way they understand. He should work the ranch instead of doing that crazy job. His father could do with someone to take over.'

The more she learned about Kendrick, the more she realised how little she knew about him.

'When are his parents due home? We'll be heading back as soon as we've passed Kip on.'

'They're due back later this afternoon. How is the boy anyway? He's up here with his mama most weekends. She rides too. Nothing like Kendrick, but not bad for a girl.'

Tim ushered Elizabeth into a chair on the veranda and left her while he went to fetch them a drink. She bounced Kip on her lap, before giving in and putting him on the floor.

'No wonder your uncle is planning to put you on a horse, young man. Looks like you're pretty fond of bouncing around.'

A cloud of dust in the distance caught her attention. As it got closer she could see it was Kendrick and Satan. He slowed the horse to a walk a few yards away and when Tim came back out with the drinks, he left them with Elizabeth and walked towards horse and rider. Kendrick swung his leg over the front of the saddle and jumped down. 'You should walk him around for a bit to cool him down. I think he'll be okay to ride now,' he told Tim.

'Very impressive,' Elizabeth said as Kendrick walked towards her.

Kendrick grinned. 'You think so? I like to impress.' He bent over and swung Kip into his arms. The little boy giggled with delight.

'Hey, Kip. What about something to eat? Then I'll take you on the horse. How does that sound?'

'You're not seriously thinking of taking him on Satan?' Elizabeth said, horrified.

'Of course not. We've plenty of well-behaved horses he can ride. Besides, he'll be with me.' He placed Kip back down on the floor, where the child found some ants to study. 'You could come too. I promise you, you'll be perfectly safe.'

Elizabeth stretched. 'Maybe later. Right now I'm just enjoying being here in the sun.'

Kendrick pulled a chair alongside hers. 'Then that's what we'll do.'

They sat in silence for a while, watching Kip as

he crawled after the ants. Every now and again Elizabeth or Kendrick had to reach down to stop him putting one in his mouth.

'Tell me about your parents,' Elizabeth asked. 'Do you see them often?'

Kendrick's expression darkened. 'Not really. I'm always travelling and, well, my father and I don't exactly get along.'

'How come? I would have thought you had a lot in common. Horses. This ranch.'

Kendrick stretched his long legs in front of him and placed his arms behind his head. Elizabeth sucked in her breath. Every part of her seemed to respond to his closeness. It was as if there was a string pulling her towards him. As if there was some kind of force field surrounding him that drew her. She had never felt like this before. Never felt every nerve cell in her body react this way to someone's presence, and it disturbed her. She'd thought she'd loved Simon, and maybe she had, but she'd never felt that constant pull towards him that she was feeling towards this man. Was this what it was like to be in love? The need to be close to someone. The feeling that the world was a darker place whenever they weren't around. The

feeling of coming home, of being at peace whenever they were. It was more, so much more than
just wanting to be in his arms or his bed.

'We were close once,' Kendrick said. 'He was
in the army and when I got into West Point he
couldn't have been prouder.'

Elizabeth waited. It was quiet, only the faint
sounds of the men shouting as they worked the
ranch disturbing the silence.

'Then when I got my helicopter pilot's licence
and was given a commission, it was as if he'd ful-
filled his life's ambition. I don't know if I said, but
he was a colonel before he retired. I knew I had
to be better than everyone else so no one could
say it was nepotism.'

Kendrick's smile was rueful. 'I wanted him to
be proud of me, so I worked my butt off. If I was
asked to run ten miles with full kit, I would run
twenty. If I was asked to do twenty press-ups, I
would do thirty. If the best got their helicopter's
licence in four months, I wanted to do it in three.
And I did.' He stood up to remove a crawling Kip
from the edge of the step. 'I made Major before
anyone else in my intake.' There was no arrogance
in the words, just a sense of certainty. 'But then,

when I was in Iraq, something happened. They busted my butt because of it. My father intervened and they agreed to put me on desk duty. But I didn't want to stay in the army to do that. If I couldn't fly, I wanted out.'

'What incident?'

Kendrick frowned. 'It's not something I like to talk about.'

'Tell me, Kendrick.' She wanted to know. She wanted to understand everything about this man. 'I can't imagine what you did to be busted.' A thought struck her. 'Unless you stole a helicopter to do a stunt?'

Kendrick gave her a slow smile and shook his head. 'I like it that you're on my side,' he said. 'And of course I didn't steal a helicopter. 'But I was in the wrong. I disobeyed orders and put my gunner's life at risk as well as the helicopter. Those babies cost millions and the army doesn't like its pilots to mess them up. And mine got pretty messed up. I was lucky to get away without a court-martial.'

That didn't sound right to Elizabeth. Kendrick was reckless, but she had seen the way he watched out for the others in his team.

Kip tottered to the edge of the step again and this time it was Elizabeth who got up to retrieve him. Her heart ached as she remembered that she'd never had to do this for Charlie. She had never crawled.

'Dad was furious,' Kendrick continued. 'He's an army man through and through. Obeying orders, being part of the team is what counts. It almost killed him that I could have been court-martialled for my actions.' A cloud passed across Kendrick's face. 'But I would do the same thing all over again if I had to.' Something in the air between them chilled.

'Dad pulled out all the stops to stop me facing a military court. Called in favours, used every bit of influence he had, and believe me that was some, to stop it. And he succeeded. So when I decided I was going to leave the army anyway, we fought.' Kendrick's lips flattened. 'Not physically, of course. Until then I had always done more or less what my father wanted. But his fury when I told him I was leaving the army was nothing compared to what he had to say when he learned I had decided to work on movies as a stuntman. He found it shameful. If I had used my pilot's licence to get a civilian flying job, he might have come around eventually, or if I'd taken over here from Tim as ranch manager, he might have lived with that. But a stuntman? In an industry he has nothing but contempt for? No way.'

'Why did you choose to become a stuntman? Why not the other options?'

'This way of life suites me. I'm considering doing some directing.' He smiled ruefully. 'One day I'll be too old to do stunts, or too injured.'

'What about the risks? Don't you care that you could get killed? Or paralysed?'

'Of course I care. But it's no more dangerous than being in the army. And as for the risks, I do the same as I did then. I try to make sure that the danger is minimised.'

He shifted in his seat. 'Enough about me. I want to know more about you. I suspect your folks were proud of you.'

'Yes, they were. My father was in the oil industry. He worked in Texas for years. He took early retirement and they moved back to England for a while. When my mother died he went to live near his sister in Canada. I was married by that time so I stayed here.'

'Where did you meet your ex-husband?'

'Simon? He worked at the oil company my father worked for.'

'Did you love him?'

'I thought I did. But I guess I didn't really know him.'

'What happened? Can you tell me?'

Elizabeth swallowed hard. 'Charlie happened.' She bent down, picked Kip up and held him tight. The familiar, sweet, precious baby smell was instantly painful. But it felt so good to hold the small bundle in her arms. Elizabeth rubbed his cheek gently with her finger.

Kip snuggled into her and yawned. He was clearly ready for his afternoon nap. She sat on the seat swing on the veranda and Kendrick sat down next to her.

Kendrick eyed the sleeping baby apprehensively. 'Ah, peace for a while. Although he is kind of cute, I have to admit I'll be glad to pass him back to his mother. Kids aren't my style. But he obviously feels comfortable with you. It must be because you're used to children.'

Elizabeth flinched and Kendrick hit himself on the forehead.

'I'm sorry, Lizzie. That was a tactless thing to say. Sometimes I'm an idiot.'

'It's okay. I need to talk about Charlie. I thought it would be better if no one knew about her so I wouldn't have to tell them what happened, but I can't pretend my daughter never existed.'

'How did she die?'

'She had a rare wasting illness called Gaucher's disease. When she was born, when I first held her in my arms I was so happy. I thought my life was prefect. Perfect husband, perfect child, perfect job. I knew I was blessed.' She smiled as she remembered the first time she'd held her daughter. The tiny rosebud mouth, the silky-soft skin, her tiny hands, the feel of her skin on her skin. 'But even as I held Charlie to me, I knew in my soul that something wasn't right. But I shook the feeling off. I told myself it was just new-mother anxiety.'

'Go on,' Kendrick prompted.

'As she got older that feeling grew stronger. I tried to tell Simon, but he didn't want to know. He was so caught up in his career I guess he thought I had too much time on my hands and that I was looking for something that wasn't there.'

'But when she should have been lifting her head,

beginning to sit up, none of that was happening. I took her to the doctor, but like Simon he told me I was being an over-anxious mother, that Charlie would do all of it in her own time. I knew they were wrong. Mothers know. We know,' she repeated.

Kendrick put his arm around her shoulder and pulled her close to him. 'I'm sorry,' he said simply.

'Eventually I got tired of everyone telling me that everything was okay when I knew it wasn't. So I took her to a private clinic. The doctor referred us straight away to a specialist children's hospital. They did tests, hundreds of them, it seemed. I can't tell you how often I wondered whether I was doing the right thing every time Charlie cried when they took blood. I felt like a monster putting her through all of that and I didn't even know whether anyone could help her.'

'Where was your husband during this time?'

'He had to work. To be fair, there wasn't much he could have done.'

'Except be with you,' Kendrick growled. 'He was Charlie's father. Your husband. It was his duty.'

'Ah, duty,' Elizabeth said softly. 'I didn't want duty. I never want duty.'

'Then what happened?'

Elizabeth's chest was tight. Although she'd told Kendrick that she needed to talk about her child, this was the first time she had talked to anyone about those awful months and it was like opening a wound and squirting acid into it.

'Eventually we got a diagnosis. Gaucher's is a genetic, irreversible wasting disease that can either affect the nervous system or muscles, or, as in Charlie's case, both.' Her throat was so tight she could hardly speak. The day she had learned for certain that Charlie's illness was both irreversible and terminal had been the worst day of her life. Simon hadn't even taken the day off work the day the doctors had given their diagnosis.

'Once I knew that there was nothing more anyone could do, I took Charlie home. Simon was livid. He thought I should have left her in hospital and then have her put in foster care. He said she was better off there. How can any child be better off without her mother? But I would have stayed with her at the hospital, I would have let them go on sticking needles in her if I'd thought there was any chance, any chance at all they could help her. As it was, all they were doing was causing my poor baby pain.'

She buried her face in Kendrick's shirt as the tears began to fall as she remembered those days—the terrible fights with Simon, the ache of not being able to help her baby.

Kendrick's hand was in her hair, and he was murmuring to her as if soothing a child.

'One day, Simon left. I woke up to find him standing at the door, with his suitcases all packed. He said he couldn't bear to watch Charlie die. That wasn't the truth. He couldn't bear it that his child was disabled. It wasn't part of the perfect image he had of himself and his life. I let him go. I didn't want him if he didn't want his own child. I stopped loving him that day. I wonder now if I ever truly loved him.'

Kendrick held a hanky underneath her nose and she took it gratefully.

'The next time I saw Simon,' she said, 'was at Charlie's funeral.'

Kendrick kicked Satan into a gallop. Elizabeth had taken Kip into one of the bedrooms and had asked Kendrick to leave her alone for a little while.

He wanted to think—no, strike that. He wanted not to think and so he was doing the only thing he knew that would stop the thoughts tumbling around his head, driving him crazy. Just as Lizzie was driving him crazy. He would have preferred to go big-wave surfing or BASE jumping, that would really have sorted his head, but he was stuck here in the desert with no waves or nearby cliffs.

So riding Satan as fast as the horse would go would have to do.

What Elizabeth had told him had shaken him. The thought of Elizabeth, his Lizzie, going through all that on her own filled him with rage. How could any man do that to his wife and child? He would never let Elizabeth face a trip to the dentist without being there for her.

How could any man leave a woman like Elizabeth? She was warm, caring and loyal even though she had been to hell and back. She had faced the worst life could throw at her with dignity and courage. He, on the other hand, had tried to run away from his guilt and loss. She was a better person than he was. A woman any man would be proud to have by his side.

The realisation hit him like a blow to the chest. He was falling in love. He didn't know when or how he had started to feel like this, but he knew he wanted to be with Elizabeth more than any other woman. He could race Satan to the back of beyond but that wasn't going to change the way he felt.

When Kendrick got back to the ranch, he still didn't know what he was going to do or say to Elizabeth, if anything. Maybe whatever this was would go away if he gave it enough time.

To his dismay, by the time he'd rubbed Satan down and walked over to the house, he saw that his parents had arrived. Hell. He wasn't expecting them back for another couple of hours at least. His mother was sitting next to Elizabeth with Kip in her arms. The two women looked as if they'd already made friends.

'Kendrick!' His mother passed Kip to Elizabeth and came across to greet him with a smile. 'It's so lovely to see you. Why does it have to take Kip to get you to come and see us?'

'Mom.' He kissed the papery cheeks and gave her a hug. 'I see you've met Dr Elizabeth Morgan?'

'Yes, Elizabeth and I have been getting to know each other.'

Uh-oh. He recognised that look on his mother's face. She was always asking him why he hadn't settled down yet.

His father came out onto the veranda and Kendrick's heart sank. Every time he and his father met, things ended in an argument. Perhaps with Elizabeth being here they could remain civil for the next couple of hours. Or perhaps he should just leave straight away. He had done what Kendall had asked and delivered Kip. He had done his duty.

'Are you staying the night, Kendrick?' The hope in his mother's eyes made him flinch.

'We need to get back to the set, Mom. Maybe another time?'

She tried to hide her disappointment, but not quickly enough. This was exactly why he didn't need or want relationships. It only brought trouble. He had to remember that.

Elizabeth stood. 'But as long as we get back before tomorrow morning, it'll be okay. Won't it, Kendrick?' Now she was ganging up on him too.

He relented. 'Sure. We'll stay for dinner, if that's okay?'

The look of delight in his mother's eyes was reward enough.

'Kendrick!' His father strode towards him with his hand outstretched. 'Good to see you, son.' They shook hands, more like acquaintances than father and son.

'Hello, Dad. Did you have a good trip?'

From the corner of his eye he could see that Elizabeth was watching the exchange with a look of bafflement on her face.

'I did. And I have some news for you. Good news.'

'I think it should wait until after dinner, Hughie,' his mother interrupted hastily.

Kendrick knew then that whatever news his father had for him, it wasn't something he wanted to hear.

'Now, why don't you watch Kip, while I show Elizabeth where she can freshen up?' his mother continued.

Kendrick managed to hold a conversation with his father long enough for Elizabeth and his mother to return. It helped that they had Kip to divert them. Kendrick had never known that toddlers required so much watching and after a few minutes of constant chasing after the lively toddler his father had suggested they saddle one of the horses and Kendrick take Kip up in front of him. It had worked like a charm. The rocking movement of the horse had sent the boy to sleep almost immediately.

'It used to work with you,' his father said. 'Mind you, you were riding on your own when you were three years old. You always refused to be led.'

It was a revelation to Kendrick. Nowhere in his memory was there an image of his father teaching him to ride.

'You had barely started at school when you were clearing jumps twice the size of yourself.'

Kendrick thought he must be mistaken. Surely that wasn't pride he heard in his father's voice?

'Come on, you two,' his mother called from the doorway. 'Supper's ready.'

It was strange sitting down to a meal with his parents in his childhood home. He couldn't remember the last time he'd done that. And even stranger seeing Elizabeth opposite him. His mother was too polite to ask Elizabeth too many searching questions, even though he could tell the curiosity was almost killing her.

'Oh, honey, I meant to tell you and I completely forgot!' Kendrick's mother, Susan, said, a look of dismay on her face.

'What is it? Is something wrong?' Kendrick replied, sounding alarmed.

But his mother was smiling widely. 'No, not wrong at all. Your Aunt Camilla phoned me while I was away to tell me that Fabio is getting married. He's finally found the girl for him. Like you should.' Susan flicked a look in Elizabeth's direction. She couldn't have made it more obvious if she tried.

'Fabio! Getting married. Well, I'll be damned. Sorry, Mother.' Kendrick turned to Elizabeth. 'My cousin Fabio is the last man I'd expect to tie the knot.'

'That's what happens, darling, when you fall in love,' his mother said with another pointed look at Elizabeth. 'They're getting married in Brazil. In three weeks' time. I know he would like you to be there.'

'I'm surprised he didn't let me know himself. Perhaps he was frightened I'd talk him out of it.'

His mother's frown told him he'd said the wrong thing. Couldn't she just accept he wasn't going to get married? 'But wild horses wouldn't keep me from Fabio's wedding. Filming should be finished by then.'

'What about you, Elizabeth? Will you go?' Susan asked.

Elizabeth gave a small shake of her head. The sad look on her face made his chest tighten. He should have kept away from her.

Finally, the meal over, Susan served the coffee.

'We should leave soon, Mom,' Kendrick said. 'If we're to make it back before midnight.'

His father cleared his throat and Kendrick knew he was ready to have his say.

'I was talking to your commanding officer a couple of days ago,' he said.

'Ex-commanding officer,' Kendrick corrected mildly.

'Yes. Well. That's the point. He wants you back. Says he's prepared to forget all about that other business.'

'I'm not going back to a desk job, Dad,'

Kendrick said tiredly. He had lost count of how many times they'd had this conversation.

'It's a good life, son. They'll give you back your rank in a year. Maybe sooner. And, besides, it's not a desk job.'

Kendrick's ears pricked up. The main reason he'd left the army had been because they wouldn't let him fly after he'd damaged their helicopter. Okay, so maybe it wasn't just because of the damage, more to do with disobeying orders, but that hadn't been the only reason he'd left.

'I'm not going back to fight in Iraq, Dad. I know you don't want to hear that.'

A look of dismay—or was it repugnance?—crossed his father's face. As a colonel and a career soldier, Kendrick's disgrace had reflected badly on him. But he was done trying to be the person his father wanted.

'They want you to come back and teach new pilots how to fly Apaches. They say no one knows how to do it better than you.'

That was different. He'd be flying again. And teaching the kids straight out of flying school how to keep themselves in one piece.

'What is an Apache?' Elizabeth asked. She'd been sitting listening quietly.

Hugh explained and Elizabeth looked even paler than she had done earlier.

'I don't know, Dad. It's a possibility. How long do I have to think it over?'

'As long as you like,' Hugh said. His smile was the first genuine one Kendrick had seen in three years. 'But he's keen to know your answer.'

'I'll think about it,' Kendrick said. He drained the last of his coffee and stood up. 'I want to ride Satan one more time before we leave, if that's okay with you, Elizabeth?'

'Sure. I'll help your mother clear away while you're gone.'

'You don't have to help,' Susan said as Kendrick and his father left the room. 'Why don't you take your coffee back outside onto the veranda? I'm used to having the kitchen to myself.'

'I'll have it at the kitchen table if that's okay?'

When Susan nodded, Elizabeth sat down and took a sip of her coffee. She liked it here. Despite the tension between Kendrick and his father, it felt comforting to be in someone else's kitchen.

'Do you think Kendrick will go back to the army?' she asked Susan.

Susan wiped her hands on a tea towel and studied Elizabeth for a moment. 'I don't know how much you know about the reason he left,' she said slowly.

'I know he got into trouble for disobeying orders,' Elizabeth replied. 'He told me.'

'Did he tell you that the reason he got into trouble was because he went to rescue a group of soldiers who were pinned down by enemy fire and that one of the soldiers who was caught in the ambush was his girlfriend Amy?'

Elizabeth was stunned. 'No, he didn't.'

Susan folded her lips as if Elizabeth's response was what she'd expected. 'Just as I thought. He doesn't talk about it to anyone.' Susan turned away and looked out of the window. 'We all loved Amy, especially Kendrick's father. We hoped that they would get married, that at long last Kendrick would settle down.'

'Loved her?' Elizabeth's throat was dry.

'She died before Kendrick could reach her. He left his helicopter to try and get to her. She was the reason he disobeyed orders. But it was no use.

He was too late. He managed to pull two other soldiers to safety, but he blames himself for not getting to Amy sooner. I sometimes think his father blames him too.'

Elizabeth's head was swirling. It explained so much about Kendrick. The haunted look she saw in his eyes when he thought no one was looking. His attitude as if every moment had to be squeezed out of life. His reluctance to get involved. Like a jigsaw, all the pieces fell into place.

'But now he's met you.' Susan turned back to Elizabeth. 'Maybe he'll have a reason to think about the future. Maybe he can find happiness again.'

It was on the tip of Elizabeth's tongue to tell Susan that she wasn't the person to bring Kendrick happiness. She had too many of her own demons to deal with, but she swallowed the words. Perhaps she and Kendrick could find some solace together, if only for a little while.

Elizabeth waited until they were a good bit along the road before she raised the question that had been bothering her.

'Your mother told me about your girlfriend,' she said.

The darkness hid Kendrick's expression from her.

'Did she now,' he said softly.

'Why didn't you tell me?'

'There was nothing to tell. I loved her. She's dead.' He couldn't hide the pain in his voice.

'So that's why you risked everything? To try and save her?'

'How the hell did anyone expect that I would leave her there? Even if I knew she was dead, I couldn't leave her.' His voice was ragged and it tore through Elizabeth. She knew his pain.

'Pull over, Kendrick,' she said.

'Why?'

'Just do as I ask.'

He pulled the car onto the side of the road and they sat in silence for a few moments.

'Is the reason you've been avoiding me anything to do with her death?' Elizabeth asked.

'Lizzie,' Kendrick said. 'Every time I look in your eyes. Every time you talk about your child, I'm reminded. And I don't want to be reminded. I want to forget.'

'Is that why you live the life you do? I know that feeling, Kendrick. I know what it's like to not want to feel. To keep your mind full so you won't think. It only works for a little while.' She reached over and took his hand in hers. 'I think what we have is good for us both. It helps us both. We'll never forget them, Kendrick, but what's wrong with finding peace where we can?'

He took a long, shuddering breath. 'I don't want to hurt you, Lizzie. You've been hurt enough.'

Reaching up, she threaded her hands behind his head. 'Nothing can hurt me any more,' she said. She pulled his face down to hers and tasted a salty wetness that made her heart ache. 'I want you, Kendrick. Even for a short while. I know once we leave here we'll go our separate ways, but for now just love me.'

CHAPTER NINE

As FILMING drew to a close, the days on the film set were quieter. Every evening, when filming had finished for the day, Kendrick saddled up Buster and they went riding. Elizabeth was delighted to find that she and her mount had developed a rapport and soon she was happy to canter for long distances.

Sometimes they stayed out after night had fallen and Kendrick would make camp. They would sit with their arms wrapped around each other, listening to the sounds of the desert. They talked a little but never of their lives. Mostly they made love. Every evening Kendrick came to her and spent the night, rising before dawn so as not to draw attention, although Elizabeth doubted they were fooling anyone. It was the happiest she had been since Charlie had died and she tried to forget that one day soon it would be all over. Kendrick would walk out of her life and she out of his and they would never see each other again.

She pushed the thought to the back of her mind. She would face the future when she had to and not a moment before. All she knew was that she wouldn't be going back to her home in the UK. It had been sold and a new family was due to move in before she got back. Elizabeth hoped they would be happy.

Jack still hadn't returned. Philip was on edge and his anxiety permeated the camp. Kendrick told her that Philip had filmed all the stunts he could, but now had to wait for Jack's return before filming could start again.

'He's worried,' Kendrick said. 'If the film goes over budget, it's his responsibility.'

'There's nothing he can do about Jack being ill.' Elizabeth did wonder though. Jack's food poisoning should have disappeared by now.

'Gossip has it that he's taken himself off to Las Vegas for a couple of days,' Kendrick said. 'Whatever, Philip can't continue until he's back. Luckily he was ahead of schedule so has a couple of days in hand before he falls behind. In the meantime, he's given everyone the weekend off. He's determined filming will start again on Monday. I suspect I'll be sent to strongarm Jack back to the set if he doesn't appear on Sunday evening.'

Kendrick studied her with a crooked smile. 'What do you say we take ourselves off for a couple of days? I'll go crazy if I have to hang around here with nothing to do.'

Elizabeth hesitated. 'What do you have in mind?'

'A day in LA, then we could drive up the coast. Remember that place I told you about? Built into the cliff? I've booked us a night.'

Still Elizabeth hesitated. She was unsure why. Perhaps it was because she could no longer kid herself that she wasn't falling for Kendrick. She felt an unexpected ache in her heart.

'Why not?'

The next couple of days were the happiest Elizabeth could remember since Charlie had died. They did all the touristy stuff in Los Angeles. Trying to fit their handprints in those of the famous film stars, walking down Sunset Boulevard.

They spent the first night in Kendrick's cabin, sitting on the beach in the moonlight, watching the surf rolling in. Kendrick sitting behind her with his legs on either side, her leaning against his chest. He taking her by the hand to his cabin where they made love, the sheets tangling in their limbs, laughing at nothing, nibbling on salt crackers and cheese.

Then setting off up the coast on Kendrick's motorbike, she holding him tightly as he whizzed along the road. Stopping for a picnic lunch of fruit, cheese and bread that Elizabeth had picked up from a delicatessen. Back on the bike with the wind in their hair.

Elizabeth was smiling when, just as evening was falling, they reached the place Kendrick had booked for the night.

The hotel was built into a mountain, the rooms set so far into the cliff they were almost invisible to the naked eye. Each one was like an isolated pod, with an open fire for cooler winter evenings and a large double bed covered in soft throws. A small plunge pool in front of their room looked out over the cliff and out to sea. Each cabin had been positioned for maximum privacy. As Elizabeth looked down on the crashing surf below an eagle flew past, almost at eye level.

She sighed. It was perfect.

'Would you like to have dinner or do you fancy a swim first?' Kendrick said. His eyes darkened as he looked at her and Elizabeth felt the familiar feeling of lust coil in her belly. She could never get enough of him. But it wasn't just lust.

When he grinned, his eyes crinkled at the corners and his eyes seemed to glint like diamonds. Whenever she was with him, it was as if the outside world disappeared and nothing mattered except that they were lost in each other.

Thinking about Charlie still made her heart splinter, but it was no longer unbearable. Instead of the all-consuming pain, she was occasionally able to think about her child without wanting to curl into a little ball and shut out the world. Was her heart at last healing a little? She would never forget her child, there was no question of that, but she was beginning to envisage a time when she could remember her daughter with gratitude for the time they'd had together. The pain, the desperate sense of loss would never go, but she welcomed the temporary lifting of the searing grief she had been carrying around with her these last few months.

Kendrick had pulled her towards him and was slowly unbuttoning her blouse, looking into her eyes all the time.

She had this man to thank for easing some of her pain.

He slipped her shirt off her shoulders and moved his attention to the top button of her jeans. Elizabeth moaned softly as he undid the button and eased her jeans over her hips.

'I think dinner and swimming might have to wait,' Kendrick said, his mouth on her belly.

As heat spiralled through her she knew that somewhere along the way, despite her resolve not to, she had fallen for this man. She was in love. For the first time in her life. What she'd felt for Simon had been nothing compared to how she felt about Kendrick. She loved him heart and soul. For ever.

The realisation chilled her to the core. This wasn't how it was supposed to be. Hadn't she told herself that the only reason she was with him was because he didn't see a future for them any more than she did?

And then as he picked her up and into his arms, all thoughts were swept away.

CHAPTER TEN

ELIZABETH looked at the faint blue line and felt ill.

Pregnant.

Definitely pregnant.

At first she'd tried to pretend that the tender breasts and nausea were signs her period was due, but as the days passed, the gnawing suspicion wouldn't go away. Then when Tara had come for her antenatal check-up, the penny had dropped. The symptoms Tara was experiencing were exactly those Elizabeth was going through.

She had been in denial. It hadn't occurred to her she might get pregnant. Charlie's conception had been almost a miracle. She was certain there was no way another one could happen. And just in case, she had put herself on the Pill. No way did she ever want to get pregnant again. She simply couldn't cope with the possibility of having another child who could die. Neither had she expected to be in a position to find herself pregnant.

After Simon she had told herself she was done with men. Yet she had slept with Kendrick and now the worst had happened.

She was pregnant. The food poisoning. Why hadn't it occurred to her that being sick might have made her contraception unreliable? Because she hadn't been thinking. At least, not with her head.

What was she going to do about it?

She got to her feet and began to pace. Although the chances of Kendrick having the defective gene were remote, it wasn't impossible. What if the same thing happened to this baby as had happened to Charlie? How could she bear to go through all that again? What, then, was the alternative? To terminate the pregnancy?

Elizabeth slid down the wall until she was on the floor. What choice was that? A termination or loving and losing another child? But this baby was another miracle. Twice in a lifetime was almost unbelievable, but three times? No, she would never fall pregnant again, even if she wanted to. Terminate this pregnancy and she would never have another child. No question.

'What should I do, Charlie?' she whispered.

'Would it have been better for you not to have lived at all than to have lived your life?'

The image of her child, smiling at her as she inspected her toes came flooding back, to be replaced almost immediately with one of her in pain. Not understanding why Mummy couldn't take the pain away. Not understanding why doctors had to poke and prod her. It was one of the reasons Elizabeth had taken her home. There had been no point in letting the doctors run constant tests on her child if it was not going to change the outcome. When she had finally made herself accept that, it had been almost liberating. Away from the hospital, at least she and Charlie had had some sort of life together. And among the sadness and grief there had been happy moments. Moments when she had held her child against her, knowing that her touch had let Charlie know she was loved.

But do it all over again?

When Simon had walked out, she'd been almost too caught up with Charlie to bring herself to care. But it had been hard and there had been many, many long and lonely nights when she had longed to have someone hold her, comfort her. She and

Simon had only moved to the sprawling London suburb a short while before Charlie's birth and over the time she'd lost touch with the friends she'd once had. Without her mother and with her father in Canada there was no family member to help.

Should she tell Kendrick? At least talk it over with him. Didn't he have the right to be involved in any decision she might make?

But what was the point? If she told him she was pregnant, he'd probably offer to support her, he was that kind of man, but he was also the kind of man who wouldn't stick around. He'd made it clear that he didn't see a wife and child in his future. Besides, if she decided not to continue with the pregnancy what was the point in telling him?

Her head was spinning.

How far on would she be? She calculated dates in her head. About five weeks. So there was time to think about what she wanted to do.

She pulled her knees to her chest and rested her head on her knees. She'd never felt so alone.

She allowed herself a few more minutes of self-pity then got to her feet and washed her face.

Hollow eyes stared back at her. Picking up her make-up bag, she applied lipstick, some blusher and mascara. Whatever was going on inside, she didn't need the world to know.

Kendrick watched as Elizabeth walked onto the set. Something was wrong. He would bet his life on it. Although she was perfectly made up, her hair falling in a curtain of liquid gold around her shoulders and she took his breath away, there was a tiny pucker between her brows, a shadow in her eyes that concerned him.

As she came closer, he could see that her eyes were a little puffy. Had she been crying? His Elizabeth?

He felt an unexpected stab of fury. Had someone said something to her? If so, he'd personally grab them by the shirt collar and shake them until their teeth shook. But that didn't ring true. Elizabeth wasn't the kind of woman to let anyone rattle her. She was too collected for that. Which made the fact that she'd been crying even more worrying.

Had she had bad news from home? A friend in trouble, perhaps?

He jumped to his feet. Whatever it was, he'd

get it out of her and then he'd be able to help. Surely there wasn't anything wrong that couldn't be fixed.

'Lizzie, honey, what is it?' He took one of her cold hands in his and rubbed it gently, wanting to get some warmth back into her. Was she ill?

She smiled but it didn't reach her eyes. It was as if she had gone to some place he couldn't reach. 'I'm fine. A bit of a headache, that's all. I've taken some painkillers, so I should be fine in a minute.'

She was lying. He was sure of it. But he'd come to know enough about this woman not to challenge her head-on. He'd get it out of her one way or another, but he'd have to leave his normally cack-handed methods and get there slowly. But get to the truth he would.

'Are you okay to work? Do you want me to tell Philip that you can't make it this evening? I'm sure he can get another doctor to fill in. This is LA after all. There's bound to be a couple of thousand who'd leap at the chance to work on a film set.'

She frowned at him and tightened her mouth in the way he knew meant she was annoyed.

'Kendrick, when will you realise that I'm perfectly capable of deciding whether I'm fit to work? I am not a child. I am not your responsibility.' She said the last words with such venom he recoiled. What had brought that on? Elizabeth might be feisty, but she was never outright rude.

'I'm sorry,' she said, and touched him on the shoulder. He had to force himself not to pull her into his arms and plead with her to tell him what was wrong. In her current frame of mind that would be exactly the wrong thing to do.

'Remind me what we're doing tonight.'

That too was unlike her. Normally Elizabeth insisted on getting the details of planned stunts in advance so she could be prepared for any eventuality. Although this part of the filming was taking place in a sectioned-off part of an LA freeway and there would be medical services close at hand should anything go wrong, she would still be the first person on the scene.

'We're doing a car chase. Josh will be crashing his car again. I'll be driving the motorbike that is trying to force him off the road.'

'Great,' said Elizabeth. 'Just what I need. You trying to get yourself killed.'

She looked so woebegone that this time he

couldn't stop himself. Uncaring that anyone could see them, he took her face between his hand, forcing her to look into his eyes. What he saw dismayed him even more. Her blue eyes were luminous with unshed tears. In that moment he knew. He was in love. Not just falling, he was deeply, irrevocably in love.

He was in a load of trouble.

'What is it, Lizzie? Please tell me.'

The silence stretched between them and as her lips moved he thought she was going to tell him. But then she shook her head and pulled away.

'You'd better get ready,' she said. 'Don't you have to get suited up?'

He dropped his hands to his sides, knowing he'd get nothing more from her. Later, when the filming was over, he'd find her and make her tell him. As for being in love? Damn. He could only hope he'd get over it when she left. He had nothing to offer her apart from a nomadic existence moving from set to set. Even if they married. Where had that thought come from? He didn't want to get married. He'd be useless at all that nine-to-five, slippers-and-newspaper routine. It would drive him crazy. And as for children, Elizabeth said she didn't want any and he believed her. But what if she changed her mind? What then? He'd be even more trapped.

But he let his mind wander. Would it be so terrible to have kids? If it was a boy, he could teach him how to ride a horse, fly aeroplanes, ride a skateboard. He could even take him surfing. Not out to the big waves, naturally. At least, not until he was fourteen. And if it was a girl? He could teach her the same things.

He let the fantasy roll around his head for a moment. He could go back to the ranch. Take over from his father who wasn't getting any younger. It could be a good life. A satisfying life. Elizabeth wouldn't need to work, but if she insisted, well, there were always shortages of good doctors in the rural parts. Suddenly the idea of being a husband and father didn't seem quite as outrageous as it once had.

He slid a glance at Elizabeth. She was chewing her lip in that cute way of hers that meant she was mulling something over. He could see her on the ranch, sitting on the rocking chair on the veranda, he sitting next to her as they talked about their day.

Kendrick forced his thoughts away from Elizabeth and his fantasies. Right now he had a big scene to do and it needed every bit of his concentration, but once filming was over for the night, he would talk to her. Find out what was bothering her and maybe even tell her he loved her.

The evening was warm as they stood around, waiting for the scene to be set up. Elizabeth tried to focus on what was happening around her instead of what was happening inside her. Every hour the cells of the baby would be dividing and multiplying as the baby developed inside her. She couldn't think of it as a baby. She mustn't think of it as a baby. Much, much better, if she had to think of it at all, was to remember it was only a cluster of cells. It wouldn't even have a beating heart yet.

'Okay,' Kendrick was saying as his team of stuntmen and women huddled around him. 'I think we're all pretty clear on how this has to work. Josh, remember to duck below the dash just before you ram into the truck. I'll be on the motorbike, next to you. We have to get the timing spot on. I don't want you knocking into me and sending me flying across the road.'

'Hey, boss, when have I ever bumped into you?' Josh said good-naturedly. 'You make sure your timing is spot on, and I'll look after mine.'

'The rest of you who aren't in this scene stand by to help Josh out of the car when it crashes. I don't want to take any chances it'll explode with him in it.'

Great. Just great. They were talking crashes and explosions and who knew what else they had planned. It would be a miracle if they all came out of this without a scratch. At least there was an ambulance with a couple of paramedics on standby as well as her. Elizabeth prayed none of the precautions she'd taken would be needed.

Over the last hour she had watched as Kendrick and Josh had set up some kind of track along the road barrier. Imogen had explained that they needed to do that in order to keep the car Josh would be driving sideways once it had been hit. It would then race along the barrier for a few hundred metres before landing back on four wheels. The rest of the crew had lined up old cars along the side of the road to act as a crash barrier on the other side.

What kind of people were these? Elizabeth wondered, not for the first time. Despite what Kendrick had told her, she couldn't accept that they didn't know that one false move could end in tragedy.

Imogen must have been thinking the same thing. Either that or she'd read Elizabeth's mind.

'We're not reckless, you know. All the stuntmen I've ever known, apart from a couple, died either from natural causes or in accidents where they weren't working.'

Was that meant to reassure her?

'You'll see. They do everything they can to make the stunt safe. And as far as I know, Kendrick hasn't lost anyone on his watch.'

They watched in silence for a little longer. 'Of course, Kendrick does like taking risks. That's why he left the army.'

Did everyone know more about Kendrick than she did?

Imogen smiled. 'I'm sure if Kendrick had wanted to stay, his father would have found a way to keep him.'

Elizabeth stayed silent, hoping Imogen would carry on musing if she wasn't interrupted.

'But I guess even the colonel couldn't get Kendrick out of trouble when it came to endangering his crew and practically writing off a multi-million-dollar helicopter. Personally I can't see what else Kendrick could have done, but I guess I'm not in the army so what do I know? All I do know is that if I were in trouble, it's Kendrick I would want to get me out of it.'

Endangering his crew? Writing off a helicopter? This was more than Susan had told her.

The more she learned about Kendrick, the more confused she became. Did she know him at all? She placed a hand over her stomach, feeling the familiar, but unwelcome, protective urge.

Josh brought Elizabeth a cup of coffee and she smiled her thanks.

'Are you sure he knows what he's doing?' she asked anxiously.

'Who? Kendrick? I trust him with my life,' Josh said simply. 'I've worked on other sets and, believe me, ones where Kendrick is the co-ordinator are the safest by far.'

'And you believe this. Even knowing why he had to leave the army?'

Josh slid her a look. 'Hey, Doc, I don't know who's been talking to you, but Kendrick only did what he had to. If I had the guts I would have done the same in his place. His girl was hit, he needed to get her out of there and he was the only one who could do it.'

'His mother told me about his girlfriend.'

Josh took a swig of coffee and studied his drink pensively. 'I doubt she knows the whole story. The horror of what he must have gone through. I'm only telling you what I've learned over the years. Kendrick doesn't talk much.' He flashed Elizabeth a smile. 'I guess you know that by now. Anyways, he was flying one of those helicopters. You might have seen them in the movies? The ones that offer support to the men on the ground?'

Elizabeth nodded.

'The way I heard it, some soldiers were involved in an unexpected ambush,' Josh continued. 'They radioed for help and Kendrick was one of them who was sent. He knew his girl was part of the platoon, but he didn't know she was dead already. It eats him up that he couldn't save her. There were a couple of soldiers who were still alive and he got them out of there while under heavy fire himself. Folk still talk about it. Trouble was, the big brass didn't see it that way. As the pilot, Kendrick wasn't supposed to leave his chopper in the hands of his gunner. The brass said any of the enemy might have got it. As it was, it took a few bullets as they were taking off. Made a mess of their expensive machine. They didn't seem to care too much about the two soldiers who almost certainly wouldn't have made it out of there alive if it hadn't been for Kendrick. I guess they didn't know whether to give him a medal or court-martial him. As it happened, his father tried to intervene. Argued that Kendrick should stay in the army but in a desk job away from the action. But Kendrick was having none of it. Said if he couldn't fly, he wasn't staying. So here he is. This way he gets to fly sometimes. I heard he and his father haven't spoken much since.'

Elizabeth was stunned. No wonder there was tension between Kendrick and his father. But his father was wrong. He should be proud of his son. Just as any child would be proud to have a father like Kendrick.

In that moment she knew. She would never terminate the pregnancy. This child would be loved, however he or she turned out.

A burst of happiness lit her up inside. She had made her decision and it was the right one.

But should she tell Kendrick? Everything she knew about him told her that he would never leave her to have the child on her own. She didn't want him to stay around out of a sense of duty. Eventually the burden of responsibility would change him, he'd feel trapped and want to leave but wouldn't. She couldn't bear to do that to him or her child.

She loved Kendrick. She would always love him. But she'd coped on her own before and she would again.

She looked over to the man who had her heart and always would, and her insides churned at the thought of leaving him. She took a deep breath and squared her shoulders. She'd make the most of any time they had left together. At least now she knew she had the strength to face the future, whatever it brought.

CHAPTER ELEVEN

THE last day of filming came round all too soon. Philip had brought in caterers for the wrap party and there was a real carnival atmosphere. Kendrick watched Elizabeth as she spoke to some of the crew, her head tilted back, laughing. She looked more beautiful than he'd ever seen her. The sadness he'd seen a few days earlier had disappeared. He'd tried to ask her about it but she'd brushed his questions away with a smile. There was a glow about her, as if she was beginning to live again. And he wanted to be part of that life. It was no use. He knew it now. He was in love with Elizabeth Morgan. Completely in love. He hadn't recognised it before because he hadn't wanted to.

It was too late to fight it. He couldn't let her leave. He couldn't imagine life without her. He wanted her to be with him for the rest of their lives. He wanted to grow old with her. For her to have his babies—the whole shooting match.

With the acknowledgement something inside him quietened down and for the first time in his adult life he felt at peace with himself. He would have to bite the bullet and ask her to marry him.

But not here. In Brazil. After Fabio and his wife-to-be tied the knot. On the beach somewhere. That was how the romantic movies did it, so it must be right. He didn't have a clue. It wasn't as if he'd ever proposed before. He would buy a ring, wait until he had her alone and go down on one knee. She would have to accept him then. A knot of anxiety tugged away at his gut. What if she said no? She'd been pretty adamant she didn't want to get married again. He dismissed the thought.

He was sure she loved him.

'Will you come with me to my cousin's wedding?' he asked as soon as he found the opportunity to get her on her own.

She looked at him with those steady blue eyes. 'In Brazil?'

'Why not? You're not rushing back to the UK, are you?'

She shook her head and he saw a shadow cross her face. No doubt she was remembering the last time she'd been there. If—no, when—she married him, he would spend the rest of his life making good memories for her.

She hesitated and the earlier knot of anxiety returned. What if he'd got it all wrong? No. It was impossible. He knew women.

'I suppose,' she said reluctantly. That wasn't exactly the response he was looking for, but it would have to do. Perhaps she was wondering what the point of dragging out their relationship was? For a second he was tempted to ask her right there and then, but he controlled the impulse. He wanted it to be perfect.

As Elizabeth stepped off the plane a fragrant breeze tickled her nostrils. They had flown to Brazil, then a smaller plane hired especially for the wedding guests had taken them out to the nearby island of Florianópolis.

The runway was only a short distance from the beach and Elizabeth saw palm trees and sand the colour of coconut milk. Whatever she'd expected, it hadn't been this.

A tall, lean man with olive skin and dark

hair stepped forward and slapped Kendrick on the back.

'Hey, Kendrick. I'm glad you could make it.'

'I wouldn't have missed my little cousin getting married for anything.' Kendrick grinned back.

Not that the man in front of her was little. Although Kendrick topped him by a good two inches, Fabio had to be six feet at least. He was good-looking, almost beautiful, but Elizabeth preferred Kendrick's ruggedness.

Green eyes turned to Elizabeth and an eyebrow was lifted in question.

'This is Dr Elizabeth Morgan,' Kendrick introduced her. 'Just don't call her Lizzie. She might take a chunk out of you.'

'I'm delighted you could come. I hope you'll enjoy your stay,' Fabio said with a quick glance at Kendrick.

'I'm sure I will.'

'So where's the bride?' Kendrick asked. 'Have I met her?' He narrowed his eyes at his cousin. 'Wait a minute. Don't tell me. I'm betting it's that cutie you were with at the film première.'

Fabio broke into a wide grin. 'And you'd be

right. She's up at my mother's right now, going over final arrangements.'

As they talked they headed out of the airport, pausing only to pick up their bags. They had cleared Immigration when they'd first arrived in Brazil.

'And how is Camilla?' Kendrick asked. 'Sounds to me as if you two have come to some sort of understanding.'

'You could say that. Katie has Mother eating out of her hand. The only problem is that she's insisting that she'll never be called Grandmother.'

Kendrick came to a halt. 'Are you...? Is Katie...?'

Fabio grinned. There was no mistaking the happiness in his eyes. Elizabeth's heart twisted. What would it be like to be loved like that? To know that you were the centre of someone's universe? Once, she too had thought the future was all mapped out and that only happiness lay ahead. How soon it had turned to dust. She shook the thought away. Hopefully life would be kinder to Fabio and his Katie.

'Yes, she's just over eight weeks pregnant. Don't

say anything, though. She's a little superstitious about it.'

Elizabeth's heart twisted again. She too remembered the excitement of being pregnant the first time but it hadn't crossed her mind to be anxious and she'd been totally unprepared for having a child with a terminal illness. Not that she would have not had Charlie in her life.

She was scared to death about this pregnancy, but this time she'd be prepared. She'd arranged for an appointment at the hospital in a couple of weeks' time. This time, if there was anything wrong with her child, at least she'd be prepared.

'I thought you could stay with us at the house,' Fabio was saying. 'I hope that's okay. Mama has invited half of the Brazilian population as well as most of the film world to the reception so accommodation is booked solid on the island. Fortunately, she's accepted that it's only close friends at the actual wedding service.'

As they pulled up in front of the house a woman ran down the steps to meet them. After a resounding kiss from Fabio, she turned to them.

'Hi, I'm Katie. It's so good to meet you again, Kendrick.'

'Me too, ma'am. This is Elizabeth.'

Katie took one of Elizabeth's arms in hers. 'Come, you must be exhausted. I'll show you to your room.' She turned around briefly. 'Be a darling, Fabio, and take the bags up to the room for our guests.'

Katie was beautiful and the added light in her eyes made her seem to glow. She was petite, only coming to Elizabeth's shoulder.

'Congratulations,' Elizabeth said as they walked up the sweeping staircase. 'You look very happy.'

'I've never been happier,' Katie said simply. She showed Elizabeth into a bedroom that was at least twice the size of her sitting room back in England. She walked over to the window and flung the shutters wide.

'We keep them closed during the day to keep the heat out. But it seems a shame to block out the view,' Katie said.

And it was some view, Elizabeth had to admit as she stepped out onto a small balcony. The beach was only a few metres away and the sea rolled gently onto the sugar-white sand.

'I wasn't sure, but do you and Kendrick want to share?' Katie asked, her grey eyes looking anxious. 'There's another room along the passage Kendrick could have.'

Elizabeth smiled. 'No, this will do perfectly.' Her heart thumped. Another couple of days and then it would be over.

'I'll leave you to freshen up. After lunch I'm afraid I'm going to have to leave you in Kendrick's hands. There's still so much to do before tomorrow. More guests—people from the practice where Fabio and I work are arriving this evening. Fabio's mother has arranged a barbecue for everyone tonight, so I'll see you there.' And then in a flurry Katie was gone.

She had just left when there was a tap on the door and Kendrick entered.

'Okay?' he asked.

'I'm fine. It's so beautiful here.'

'Fabio is a lucky man,' Kendrick said. 'Things haven't always been easy for him.'

'Why?'

Kendrick took her by the arm and they went out onto the balcony. Elizabeth rested her back against his chest, savouring the feeling of his arms around her, wanting to make the most of every last minute they had together.

'He hasn't always got along with his mother. Remember I told you about his parents on the plane out here?'

When Kendrick had told her that Fabio's parents were Camilla Salvatore and Tom Lineham, Elizabeth had immediately known who they were. Tom Lineham, although dead for many years, was still a legend.

'Fabio's childhood was pretty isolated. I never thought he'd fall in love and settle down. His relationship with his father—my mother's brother—was fraught even before my uncle died. A bit like mine with my father.'

He rested his chin on the top of her head. 'Speaking of which, I'm seriously considering going back to the army.'

Elizabeth's blood ran cold. It was one thing her making plans for a future without him, quite another to hear him doing the same. She only prayed he wouldn't be going back to the front line.

'If you do, will you go back to active service?' she asked.

'I'm not sure. At this stage, it's only tentative. I haven't said yes—yet. I'd like to train other pilots. But once I'm back in the army they can send me where they like. And anyway,' he said thought-fully, 'I don't know if I could train pilots without flying with them on missions.'

This was worse than anything she'd expected. Over the time she'd watched Kendrick work, she'd come to realise that he managed the risks and while the stunts were still dangerous, at least they were carried out in controlled conditions with her close by to help if she were needed. Out there, there was no way to control the risk. She swallowed the lump in her throat. She wouldn't say anything. What was the point? Kendrick had made it clear that he didn't want the responsibility of worrying about someone else and she knew instinctively that he wasn't the kind of man to change his mind once it was made up. Maybe it was for the best they were never going to see each other again. She couldn't bear the thought of someone else she loved dying.

'Fabio wants me to go and play polo with him this afternoon. Would you like to come and watch?'

Elizabeth shook her head. She needed time alone so she could absorb what Kendrick had just told her. Fixing a smile on her face, she turned in his arms and pulled his head down towards hers. 'What time is lunch?' she asked.

Kendrick glanced at his watch behind her back. 'Not for another hour.'

'In that case,' she whispered, raising her mouth to his, 'I think we have just enough time.'

After lunch Kendrick headed out with Fabio. The memory of Elizabeth in his arms made him smile. Then he frowned. There had been something desperate in their love-making this time, something urgent, as if she had been trying to memorise every line and plane of his body. She didn't know yet, of course, that this wasn't goodbye. For a moment, when he'd told her about possibly going back to the army, he'd been tempted to propose, to tell her that he wouldn't go unless she could go too, but he'd held back, not wanting to spoil his planned proposal.

There was no time to think too much about it as shortly after they reached the polo field they were mounted and, on the opposing team from his cousin, soon immersed in their game.

Later, after they had showered and the other

players had gone, Kendrick decided to share his plans with Fabio.

'You're not the only one who's going to get married,' Kendrick said. The look on his cousin's face was priceless.

Fabio slapped him on the back. 'Why didn't you say before? I would have congratulated Elizabeth.'

'She doesn't know. Not yet. I'm going to spring it on her tomorrow. After your wedding. I didn't want to steal your thunder. I've done that too many times in the past.'

Fabio grinned back. 'I think the score is pretty even, mate. Although you're bound to catch up soon. I don't go surfing and BASE jumping so much any more. I've somehow lost the urge. Falling in love and becoming a father tends to do that. I kind of realise that I can't take the risks we used to. I have responsibilities now.'

He grinned again and although Kendrick had never thought he'd hear the word 'responsibility' uttered by Fabio with a smile, he knew how his cousin felt. Was it fair to be thinking of proposing to Elizabeth if he might go back to the front line? He had the uneasy feeling it wasn't. He only hoped she would understand.

CHAPTER TWELVE

IT WAS a perfect day for a wedding, Elizabeth thought as she stepped out onto the balcony. Kendrick was still sleeping, his arms and legs splayed out in careless abandon.

It had been late when he'd come back last night and he had crept into bed quietly so as not to wake her. He wasn't to know that she had been staring wide-eyed at the ceiling until she'd heard his footsteps outside the door. For once she'd pretended to be asleep. She hadn't been able to bear him to read the truth in her eyes.

A cool breeze rustled the palm trees. One more day and they would be saying goodbye. She was flying back to London to see her obstetrician.

She shivered and hearing footsteps behind her turned to see Kendrick, completely comfortable in his nakedness, coming towards her. Wrapping his arms around her, he hugged her close.

'You're cold,' he said. 'Come back to bed so I can warm you.'

But even as she gave herself up to him, she wondered if she'd ever feel warm again.

The wedding was a simple affair but no less moving for that. The bride wore a simple dress in a gauzy, almost diaphanous material with her hair in a chignon. The groom was in a white shirt and white linen trousers.

The service was held under a palm tree on the beach in front of Camilla's home. True to form, the groom's mother sniffed her way through the service. As the bride's father was no longer alive, Kendrick gave her away to Fabio. The permanent grin on his face was even wider, if that was possible.

As Katie and Fabio made their vows to each other, Elizabeth had to blink tears away. The couple were so much in love and had the rest of their lives together.

Elizabeth's mind strayed to the life growing inside her. In a different world the couple standing before her could have been Kendrick and herself, the baby growing inside her a source of happiness and joy, instead of fear and anxiety. At that moment she knew. She had to tell Kendrick. Whatever she decided to do, he had the right to know.

After the photographs and the toasts everyone made their way back to the house where the wedding feast was to be held. After that there would be dancing and the couple would be leaving for the airport. Apparently they were to honeymoon in Istanbul, a city that had special meaning for them.

As Elizabeth was about to follow the other guests back to the house, Kendrick appeared by her side.

'Elizabeth, will you walk with me?' The unusually formal language and the out-of-character nervousness on his face made her wonder.

'Sure,' she said, and as he took her hand in his she let herself be led along the beach. They walked in silence. Several times Kendrick opened his mouth as if to say something, then closed it again. Suddenly Elizabeth had had enough. She had to tell him now. Before she lost her courage.

'I'm pregnant, Kendrick,' she blurted.

'Pregnant?' He seemed stunned.

Oh, my God. This was harder than she'd expected. Deep down, she wanted him to be happy, to be delirious. To love them both.

She turned to face him, her eyes searching his. If only she could see a glimmer of joy in his face, if only…

Then his mouth split into a wide grin. 'Pregnant? When, how, what…?' His hand reached over and gently rubbed her stomach. 'We're having a baby?'

Elizabeth nodded.

The look of wonder in his eyes almost ripped her in two. 'That's great, Lizzie.' He picked her up in his arms and whirled her round.

Then, to her amazement, he dropped to one knee and looked up at her.

'I feel like such an idiot down here.'

He looked so woebegone that Elizabeth swallowed the bubble of laughter that rose to her throat.

'Elizabeth Morgan,' Kendrick said, taking her hand, 'would you do me the very great honour of becoming my wife?' He rose to his feet and smacked the sand off his trousers. 'Sorry. Can't do the kneeling thing. Doesn't do it for me. There's only one way to do this that feels right.'

He dropped his hands to her waist and she swayed towards him. He looked her directly in the eye and she saw hope and fear and love there.

'I love you. I never thought I'd say that, but I do. I want you to be my wife.'

She knew what she wanted to say, but she couldn't. Had he only proposed because she was pregnant? What if he walked away, like Simon, leaving her on her own? She couldn't go through all that again. She simply wasn't strong enough.

He was waiting for her answer.

'No, Kendrick, I'm sorry, I can't.'

He frowned. Clearly her reply wasn't what he was expecting. 'What do you mean, you can't? You love me, don't you?'

Elizabeth ran a hand across his face. 'I don't think you realise what the implications of this pregnancy are. This baby—our baby—might be born with the same condition that my darling Charlie had. Can you cope with that?' She dropped her hand, tears welling in her throat.

Kendrick's fingers bit into her shoulders. His eyes burned into hers. 'I'm not Simon. I'll never be like Simon—you have to believe me, Lizzie. You mean more to me than my own life—and if our child is less than perfect, we'll see it through. Together. I promise you that.'

She wanted so much to believe him. Wasn't love about trust? Elizabeth wrapped her arms around his neck and he hugged her with such ferocity she thought he'd never let her go. Then he was kissing her, sweet, desperate kisses. So this was what real love felt like.

Nevertheless, although it broke her in two, she knew what she had to do. She pulled away.

'Love you, Kendrick?' She made herself frown. 'I thought I made it clear from the start that this wasn't going to end in happy-ever-after?'

He laughed harshly. 'That was then. We both said things but that was before we knew we were going to fall in love.'

There was a glint in his eye, the beginning of a hardness she couldn't bear to see. But she knew she had to twist the knife one more time.

'I'm not in love. And I suspect you aren't, either. Not really. You're thinking of going back to the army after all. You decided to do that without talking to me. Don't you think, Kendrick, that was a decision you should have discussed with the woman you purport to love?'

His eyes narrowed. The smile was gone. 'So that's what this is about,' he said softly. 'Me going back to the army. Maybe I should have talked to you first,' he said, 'but I'm used to making my own decisions. It's a habit. I'll get used to consulting with you in time.'

Elizabeth stepped back. 'I'm sorry, Kendrick. I don't know what gave you the idea I could marry you. And if you think I'm going to wait at home, worrying that you might get killed, you have another think coming.'

'So that's what this is about, Lizzie.' The darkness in his eyes cleared. 'I'm an idiot. Of course, given what happened with Charlie, you're bound to be more worried about me. But don't you know by now? I can look after myself.'

She reached across and opened the button of his cotton shirt. She found the bullethole and circled it with her finger. 'Like you looked after yourself then? You could have been killed that day. You have a death wish, Kendrick, and no one is going to get that out of you. Least of all me.'

Her throat was getting tighter and she could

hardly bear to look him in the eyes. If he saw them, he would know she was lying.

'I need to know if this baby has the slightest chance of having the same syndrome Charlie had,' she said. 'So, if you do love me, there is one thing you can do for me. I have an appointment with a geneticist at a specialist children's hospital. Meet me there. He'll need a blood sample from you as the father. If, after having time to think about being a husband and a father to a possibly disabled child, and you decide that's still what you want, we can talk again.'

'I won't change my mind, Lizzie,' he said. 'You should know me by now. I'd follow you back to England right now if I could, but I can't. Philip needs me back in LA for a couple of days to review the film of the stunts, but after that, nothing will keep me away from you or our baby.'

Elizabeth wanted to believe him. If he'd proposed to her before she'd told him about the baby, perhaps she would have. Giving him a way out was the right thing to do. If, after time apart, he still wanted her and their baby, maybe she'd let herself trust in him.

She turned away. 'I'm going back to the house,

Kendrick. And from there I'm catching the first plane back to London. You take your time and think long and hard before deciding to come to London.'

He pulled her back into his arms.

'I'll be there, Lizzie. I promise.'

CHAPTER THIRTEEN

KENDRICK smiled. In a couple of days he'd be with Elizabeth and he was never going to leave her or their baby again. At least, not if he could help it. Sure, there would be times when he'd have to go away—he had to work—but he'd made sure the weeks after the baby was born he'd be free to spend every minute with his new wife and child.

If Elizabeth thought he would ever abandon his child, regardless of how it turned out, she didn't know him. Not that he could blame her. Up until he'd fallen in love with Lizzie, a wife and child hadn't figured in his plans. Now there wasn't anything he wanted more.

They would get married as soon as possible. He didn't care where, that was up to Elizabeth. They could get married on the moon if she wanted. He would spend the rest of his life making sure she had whatever she wanted. These last couple of weeks had been the longest of his life.

He checked his parachute and his buckles one more time. It was unfortunate that Philip had wanted to reshoot the stunt, but the director had been right. The scene wasn't perfect and Kendrick wasn't happy with anything less.

Philip had asked him again whether he would be second director in the next movie. It would mean not taking up the training position with the army and less actual stunt work, but it was an interesting proposition. He would wait until he'd spoken to Elizabeth before making his decision.

He smiled again. Who would have thought that he would be glad that he had someone to talk over decisions with? He'd always made up his mind without having to consult anyone else. But this felt good—and right.

'Ready when you are, Kendrick,' Philip shouted. The megaphone screeched in the silent desert air.

Kendrick climbed into the car. It was the same routine as before. He'd wait until the second the car went over the cliff, with him clearly visible at the wheel, then he'd scramble out the removed rear window and jump away. It required split-second timing, but he'd done it before without mishap. It was a dangerous stunt, one only a few of the most experienced stuntmen would even attempt, but he had all the skills it required. It might be his last stunt, so he'd make sure this one was perfect. Then he could get home, throw his few belongings into a bag, including the teddy bear he'd bought for the baby, and head for the airport.

'Okay, let's roll,' Philip shouted.

Kendrick grinned. Life was good.

When Kendrick opened his eyes he was in hospital. At least, that was where he thought he was. His mother was sitting by his bed, looking pale and frightened.

All he could remember was redoing the stunt with the car going over the cliff and then struggling to open his parachute, which had somehow become tangled…then nothing.

He tried to reach out to his mother, to touch her and take away the bleak look in her eyes, but he couldn't. He couldn't move anything. It was as if he was trapped inside some kind of torture device.

A nurse leaned over him and cool, practised hands touched his forehead. 'You're awake, then,' she said. 'I'll go and get the doctor.' She scurried out before he had a chance to say anything.

His mother leaned over and kissed his cheek. Standing behind her was his father. If he didn't know better, he would have sworn he saw tears in his father's eyes.

'Why am I here?' Kendrick asked.

'Try to keep still,' his mother whispered.

He almost laughed. He couldn't move if he tried.

More images came back to him. The desperate attempt to open his parachute, knowing he had only moments left. The sickening sensation of slamming against the side of the mountain. Then nothing.

'Why can't I move?' Even as he said the words, a terrible realisation was dawning.

'You hurt your spine in the fall,' his mother whispered. 'They don't know how badly. Not yet.'

A chill was seeping into his bones. This is what he'd always dreaded. What all stuntmen and women dreaded. The thing they never talked about. The thing that was worse than death.

Where was Lizzie? There was something about Lizzie he had to remember but he couldn't.

He closed his eyes.

When he came to again, his parents were still there. His mother was pretending that she hadn't been crying and his father was talking to the doctor in a low, urgent voice. There were dark circles under his mother's eyes. She should go and get some rest. Hadn't he told her to go?

'Could I ask you all to leave us for a moment?' A masculine voice came from his left. Kendrick turned his head—at least that was one part of his body he could move. The voice came from a man about his age dressed in blue hospital scrubs.

Reluctantly his visitors stood. 'We'll be just outside the door,' his father said gruffly, and placing his arm around Susan's shoulders led her out of the room.

'I'm Dr Urquhart,' the figure introduced himself. 'How much do you remember of what happened?'

CHAPTER FOURTEEN

ELIZABETH waited outside the doctor's consulting-room.

Whenever the doors of the clinic swished open she'd look up, expecting to see Kendrick striding towards her, and every time it wasn't him her heart sank.

She glanced at her watch for the hundredth time. Ten past four. The appointment had been for four o'clock.

The feeling of dread was growing stronger. Why wasn't he here? Had he decided after all that, however slim the chances were of having a disabled child, he couldn't cope? He had phoned once since they'd left Brazil and after that—nothing. When he'd phoned he'd been certain he was coming.

Elizabeth twisted the handkerchief between her fingers. She'd been right to trust her instincts. Two weeks apart had been enough for Kendrick to re-alise that even if he did love her—and she could have sworn that he did—he couldn't commit to the responsibilities of being a husband and father.

She shifted in her seat. She'd been so sure he loved her. But had she really believed it? Wasn't that exactly the reason she'd imposed this time-out? Because she wanted him to be a hundred per cent certain? Because she couldn't bear to go through again what Simon had put her through?

She'd been crazy to allow herself to hope. She should have known that it had all been too good to be true. As soon as he'd had time to think about the pregnancy, he'd got cold feet, just as she'd feared he would.

She brought her hands to her stomach. It didn't matter. Kendrick or no Kendrick, this baby would be loved with all her soul. But it hurt. She'd let herself believe in Kendrick. Let herself think that he was different. That he wasn't the running-away type, and she had been wrong.

A tall shape paused behind the frosted glass of the double doors and Elizabeth's heart leaped to her throat. Kendrick! He was here. He was late, that was all. She should never have doubted him.

As happiness soared through her, she stumbled to her feet, ready to fling herself into his arms.

But as the doors swung open and it wasn't Kendrick her heart crashed again. All of a sudden with a certainty that stole her breath she knew he wasn't coming.

Everything blurred and she felt behind her for the seat. He wasn't coming. He didn't love her enough. She had to accept that. She cupped her stomach with her hands, feeling a primeval surge of protectiveness.

'It's just you and me, darling,' she whispered. 'But we'll be okay.' Whatever and however this baby turned out, she would love it with every fibre of her being.

Six months later, Elizabeth stood back and surveyed her handiwork. Not bad. She'd decided on pale yellow paint for the walls. That way, whether it was a boy or a girl, all she'd have to do would be to add accents in the appropriate colour. It was hard to believe she'd been back in the UK for two months, having spent four months of her pregnancy with her father in Canada.

She had found this place after a couple of weeks of searching and although it wasn't perfect, it would do her and the baby for the time being.

As the baby moved inside her, she placed her hands on her abdomen. 'Hey, something tells me you're going to be like your daddy. Never happy unless you're on the move.'

The thought of Kendrick brought a lump to her throat. She still loved him—even though he'd hurt her more than he'd ever know. But she couldn't wallow in her misery or self-pity—she'd a baby to think about. Her doctor had told her that Kendrick had tested negative as a carrier of Gaucher's disease. But that was all he could say. At least Kendrick had kept that promise. Not that the result made any difference. Even if Kendrick had tested positive, she wouldn't have changed her mind about having the baby.

She picked up the photograph of Charlie and smiled. Although the memory of her daughter still made her heart ache, at least she could think of her without the heart-breaking sadness of before.

'Hey, Charlie,' she whispered, 'do you think your brother or sister is going to like their room?'

The air ambulance service had hired her and she was to take up her post six months after the baby was born. By that time she would need to have sorted some sort of help. There was no room in the flat for a live-in nanny, but if she was careful, she could afford to pay someone to come in Monday to Friday. She could manage. All this child really needed was love…and she had plenty of that to give.

As usual her mind turned to Kendrick. What was he doing? Had he gone back to the army? Was he even now on the front line or training pilots somewhere closer to home? She pushed the thought away. Kendrick was out of her life.

Taking the paintbrush with her, she walked into her kitchen. Suddenly she felt a twinge in her abdomen. It was ten days earlier than her expected due date so it was likely it was Braxton-Hicks' contractions. But the baby could be on its way. At least she had finished painting the nursery. Her bag had been packed for a couple of weeks now. All she had left to do was assemble the cot.

Back in the nursery she surveyed the pieces with dismay. Then she gritted her teeth, picked up the instructions and set about her task.

The cot was almost half-completed when she heard a ring at the door. It was probably the postman with the stuff she'd ordered from the baby shop.

The doorbell rang again, more insistently, followed by loud banging.

'I'm coming,' she called, pushing a lock of hair behind her ears.

When she opened the door her heart crashed against her ribs.

'Lizzie. Can I come in?' Kendrick said.

Unable to speak, she stood back and without waiting for an invitation he stepped into her small hall. He was thinner than she remembered, but it wasn't that that caught her attention. He was limping and leaning heavily on a cane. She had to grip her hands together to stop herself reaching out to him.

'What are you doing here?' she asked. But Kendrick, never one to let a lack of an invitation stop him, walked into her lounge. He sat himself down on her sofa and stretched his legs in front of him. He winced.

Elizabeth hid her anxiety. How had he hurt himself?

'You're looking well, Lizzie,' he said. She couldn't read the look in his eyes.

'I'm fine. The baby's fine.' Another twinge, more like a real contraction this time, squeezed her abdomen. 'How did you find me?'

Kendrick grinned and her heart somersaulted. She'd hoped that by now she'd have got over him a little. The way her pulse was beating told her otherwise.

'With great difficulty,' he said. 'But eventually I tracked you down though the employment records of the film company.'

'That information is supposed to be confidential.'

'Ah, Lizzie. Don't you know there are ways and means if you want something badly enough?'

'You had no right, Kendrick. And you still haven't told me why you're here. If your conscience has got the better of you, please don't worry. As you can see, I'm doing fine.'

He glanced over at the cot, which was standing in the same lopsided position as she'd left it. She never had been much good with reading instructions.

'I can see that.' He stood and limped across to the cot. 'You haven't done so well with this.'

Tears of fury pricked her eyes. Who did he think he was, coming in here and making her feel all sorts of stuff she didn't want to feel?

'I want you to leave,' she said through gritted teeth. Just then another contraction ripped through her body and she turned away so he wouldn't see her grimace. But he was too busy taking the cot apart and reassembling it to notice.

'What happened to your leg?' she asked, curiosity getting the better of her. 'Did you crash your helicopter?'

'Not exactly,' he said. 'Give me a minute, will you?'

Give him a minute? He had five before she should call the hospital.

'Kendrick, I want you to leave,' she said again. Then another pain sliced through her and this time she couldn't help the involuntary cry that slipped out.

'Lizzie. Is it the baby?' Instantly he was by her side and easing her into a chair.

'Say what you have to then leave me alone,' she snarled through gritted teeth. As another contraction seized her, her nails dug into his arms. God, the contractions were coming too soon. No more than three minutes apart. If she didn't want the baby born here, she had to get to the hospital.

'Explanations can wait,' he said grimly. 'First I think we need to get this baby delivered.'

* * *

He insisted on taking his car, which he had parked outside. Carefully he helped her into the front seat.

'My bag,' she gasped. 'I left it upstairs.'

He took one look at her. 'I'll get it later,' he said. 'Which hospital?'

Clearly he thought he was driving a stunt car, Elizabeth thought between the pains cramping her body. Kendrick was driving as if he was being chased by a man with a machine-gun, overtaking when he had the slightest gap and going up on the pavement to pass stationary cars. It would be a miracle if they weren't stopped by the police.

'Slow down or you'll kill us all,' Elizabeth ground out between clenched teeth.

But it seemed as if Kendrick was determined to beat the record for crossing London. Before Elizabeth knew it, they were pulling up outside the maternity unit of the hospital she had booked into and Kendrick was demanding that someone bring a wheelchair and a doctor right this second.

'My girl is having a baby. Our baby,' he told the porter who arrived with a wheelchair. The look of pride and fear on his face would have made Elizabeth laugh if she'd been less angry with him and in less pain.

'I'm not his girl,' Elizabeth told the porter as he steered the chair into the hospital. 'He's just some madman. Tell him to go.'

'It's all right, love,' the porter said. 'A lot of mothers blame the bloke at this point. You'll see— once you have the baby, you'll feel differently.'

'I will not feel differently in a hundred years,' she said. 'He didn't bother to turn up to the doctor's appointment six months ago. This is the first time I've seen him since.'

The porter glanced across at Kendrick and frowned disapprovingly.

'I was in hospital, mate. I couldn't get out of bed, let alone make it to the appointment.'

In hospital? This was the first Elizabeth had heard of it. No doubt Kendrick was trying to find excuses to make himself look better in the porter's eyes, but this was going too far.

'Even if that's true...' she glared at Kendrick as another contraction hit her '...there are telephones. Mobiles even. I think they have them in the US too?'

Nurses were coming towards them. Hands were reaching out. They were asking her questions. How long had her contractions been coming? How far apart? Her partner could have a seat outside while they examined her to see how far along she was.

'My husband?' Elizabeth spat. 'He's the last man on earth that I will ever call my husband.'

Then she was on a bed and they were giving her gas and air. A couple of lungfuls and she started feeling as if she was floating above herself. When she looked around, Kendrick was standing over her, smiling. Who had let him in? Hadn't she said she didn't want him here? This was her baby. Kendrick could have visitation rights. Maybe. Once he proved he could be a reliable father.

'You're doing fine, Lizzie,' Kendrick was saying. 'It looks like our baby is going to be born quite soon.' Kendrick was wearing a green gown and mask. All she could see were his blue eyes.

The nurse injected something into her thigh and the euphoric feeling got better.

'Hey, did I ever tell you that I love your eyes?' Elizabeth said out loud. Where had that come from? She didn't like anything about the lying, miserable no-good man in front of her who had chickened out when he'd known she was having his baby. His baby, who for all he'd known at that time, could be born with a terrible illness.

'You know this baby is okay, don't you? You found out, and you decided it would be quite cute to have a child after all for the occasional trips to the park. Wait a minute…' She wagged a finger at him. 'You probably want help on the ranch, is that it? Maybe you want to teach him or her to fly a helicopter.'

Crazy words were coming out of her mouth but she couldn't stop them.

'Is that it? Men like you always decide sooner or later that they want a kid. Some kind of macho need to spread your genes, and even better if you don't have to take responsibility.' She was proud of the way she managed to put emphasis on the last word. If he had a modicum of intelligence he'd remember that she'd told him quite clearly, once, that she didn't need or want him to be responsible for her.

'I'm here because I love you. I want to marry you. Have babies with you.'

Now she was hallucinating.

'Hah! You can't fool me,' she said. 'I may be drugged up to the eyeballs and I may be in love with you...' Double oops. She had slipped up badly that time. 'I mean, I may have thought I was in love with you, but I was wrong.' Now she'd forgotten what she was going to say. Something about him being in love with her. Something about how that couldn't be right.

''Cause if you loved me, you would have come to the hospital, or if something stopped you, you could have phoned me,' she continued. At least he could have. Up until a month ago when she'd lost her mobile and had had to get a new number. But that had been five months after he'd promised to meet her. No one took five months to work out whether they loved someone enough to risk having a child who might not be perfect with them.

'I couldn't come before, Lizzie,' he said, so quietly she had to strain to hear the words. 'I came as soon as I could, I promise.'

'I think we're going to have a baby,' the nurse said from somewhere down between Elizabeth's legs.

Kendrick stepped towards the end of the bed and Elizabeth grabbed him by the hand. 'Oh, no, you don't, mister. You're not going anywhere south of my head. So unless you want to be kicked out for sure, don't you dare move a muscle.'

Thirty minutes later, Elizabeth was holding her son in her arms. He was perfect. His mouth like a rosebud, tiny fingers and toes all accounted for, and blue eyes, although of course that could change.

Kendrick was gazing at his child with a look of wonderment on his face.

'Is he...?' He cleared his throat. 'Is he all right?'

For a moment Elizabeth wondered what he meant. 'Do you mean you don't know?' she said. 'But you gave a blood sample to be tested. Didn't you get the results?'

Kendrick shook his head. 'I didn't want to know. I never doubted I'd love our child, perfect or not. But until I knew I could be a father, I knew I had to stay out of his life. Both your lives.'

'What do you mean?' Elizabeth kissed the wispy hair on her son's head as he suckled. The nurses had left them on their own, promising to come back in a little while to check up on mother and son.

'The reason I didn't meet you as I promised is because I was in hospital.'

Elizabeth looked up from her child, seeking the eyes of the man she knew she would never stop loving.

'What happened?' she asked.

'Remember I told you in Brazil that I needed to go back to California?'

Elizabeth nodded.

'Philip decided he needed to do the car-off-the-cliff stunt again. Something went wrong. I was pretty badly hurt.'

Elizabeth felt her heart squeeze. He'd been hurt and she hadn't even known.

'I had a compressed fracture of the spine and they thought I might not walk again,' Kendrick said. 'I knew then that I couldn't come to you. I couldn't put you through all that again. Caring for me like you had to care for Charlie. I love you too much to do that to you.'

'You should have told me!' The cry was wrenched out of her. Kendrick had been hurt, had needed her and she hadn't been there. 'I would never have left you on your own. I would have

looked after you. You should have trusted me.'
And she should have trusted him.

The look he gave her was one of ineffable sadness. 'I know you would never have left me, Lizzie. That's why I couldn't tell you.'

He sat on the bed next to her and pulled her into his arms.

'I wanted to be with you. I wanted to be a father to our baby. It was what gave me the strength to fight. I wouldn't give up. Every small movement I regained brought me closer to you and our child.' He looked down at their baby and smiled.

'It took me all this time to learn to walk again,' he said. 'But I did it. When you walk down that aisle to become my wife, I wanted to be standing there waiting for you. On my feet. Without support.'

'But isn't that what people who love each other do, Kendrick?' she said. 'Support each other? In sickness and in health? The works?'

'It's what you do and what I would do for you. But can you try and understand why I couldn't come to you before now? It's because I love you that much I would rather walk away than see that love diminished over time as you cared for me.

I'm not the kind of man who could accept that. I wanted you to have me whole or not at all.'

Her heart was beating fast within her chest. He loved her. She knew that now. He loved her as much as she loved him. There would be no more leaving, no more doubts, only certainty and love.

She looked up at him. 'What does a woman need to do to get kissed around here?' she said.

EPILOGUE

ELIZABETH bent and placed a posy of flowers on her daughter's grave. Kendrick was standing a step behind her, holding their baby in his arms. Tomorrow they'd be going back to the States. Kendrick's leg would never heal well enough for him to go back to the army. Flying helicopters demanded peak physical condition and it was likely he'd always walk with a limp. He wouldn't be going back to stunt work either. Instead, he'd be working behind the scenes as a second director, with full control over organising and ensuring the execution of the stunts. He'd told Elizabeth that it had always been part of his plans.

She had told the ambulance service that she wouldn't be coming to work for them after all. When baby Josh was old enough, she would probably retrain as an emergency specialist. It was what she enjoyed doing most.

She stepped back and took their baby from

Kendrick, holding her child close, knowing that this one would never replace the one she had lost. Kendrick pulled her against him and she leaned against him, savouring his strength and his love.

'Sleep tight, my darling Charlie,' she whispered. 'Mummy will never forget you.'

She stood in the circle of Kendrick's arms, holding their child, and as the wind pushed the clouds away and the sun beat down on her shoulders she knew that life was going to be good.

* * * * *